Landscape with Figures

Landscape with Figures is the story of the children, the women and the men who live within the invisible boundaries of a catchment area in East Anglia – people whose fortunes may or may not be intertwined, but who all belong to the same country scene. Through the eyes of the headmaster, the local doctor or two young reporters, for instance, we see into the happenings of a complete community – the ups and downs of young families, the struggles and achievements of the middle-aged, the fears and satisfactions of the elderly, even the observations of passing strangers. We are shown not only how they all tick over, but why they tick over, and the repercussions which the high and the mighty produce when they begin to make laws and bye-laws and generally throw their weight about.

Doreen Wallace has written over forty novels and her latest reveals once more her unrivalled knowledge of East Anglian folk, her incomparable understanding of a county's problems, and her eye for the daily dramas of life in England today.

by the same author

Landscape
with Figures

DOREEN WALLACE

COLLINS   St James's Place, London   1976

William Collins Sons & Co Ltd
London Glasgow Sydney Auckland
Toronto Johannesburg

First published 1976
© Doreen Wallace 1976
ISBN 0 00 222357 0

Set in Monotype Times

Made and Printed in Great Britain by
William Collins Sons & Co Ltd, Glasgow

Contents

Author's Note

None of these many people is a portrait. A bit from here and a bit from there, and one puts together a more interesting and coherent character than that of a real person. Coherence is necessary because a novel has a limited number of words in which to tell a great deal of story, whereas a living man has a lifetime for doddling around 'finding himself', as they say.

The events in this book, however, are mostly true or on the way to becoming true. Funny-peculiar times we live in, even in the country. Though our two cub reporters find life in their catchment area one long yawn, those who have to live there find it a test of endurance. Some pass the test, some fail. Only the young can escape – and they might be sorry. The rest of us endure: and prefer the country to the high-rise city.

There's no choice for the true countrymen, the farmers and farm-workers. Their life and their work are in this catchment area and they don't complain. Life is not dull when you are busy all the time and can feel that your work is productive and necessary. Tiring, frustrating, maddening maybe – so much of it dependent on the totally uncontrollable weather – but not boring.

DOREEN WALLACE

1
Jimmy and Jane

On a hot sunny day, a rare day in an East Anglian June, a small elderly woman, pretty, carefully made-up and rather lame, hurried up and down the few streets of the little market-town and suddenly fetched up against a large young policeman, who put out a hand to stop her as she was about to step from the narrow pavement into the traffic-filled (and also narrow) carriageway.

'Oh, officer,' she panted, 'you haven't seen my brother, have you? A tall smiling man, a smooth face, not a care in the world?'

The intelligent young constable thought there was something a bit off in the last few words. Obviously this nice little lady had lots of cares, even her make-up could not conceal her wrinkles, and she was in quite a tizz about this oddly carefree brother.

'Would I know him, ma'am? Do you live in Radmere?'

'Oh, no, six miles off. But I bank here and I have to bring him because I can't leave him, and he's probably forgotten where I parked my car.'

'Could I have your name and address, for the record, ma'am?'

'I am Mrs Peters, Fen Lodge, Oldgrave, and my brother is Mr James Holly of the same address. It's so sad, officer, he was chairman of a company but his mind went, and now he lives with me and I've lost him, only temporarily I'm sure, but I'm tired out with running up and down the streets. You see, he may have popped into a shop just before I spotted him; more than once though he hasn't any money – '

'What age is this gentleman, madam?' (Clearly a nutter, whatever his age, but the little lady was equally clearly entitled to be called Madam.)

'Eighty-seven,' she said: then rapidly added as though to correct a misstatement, 'He's the eldest of a long family and I'm the youngest. I'm very far short of him, the poor old lad.'

The policeman, though young, knew exactly why she had made this supplementary statement. He must not be allowed to suspect that the sister of an old codger of eighty-seven was herself approaching that age. If he did, he and his mates would be in duty bound to watch her driving, and at her slightest mistake, put her off the road until she passed a driving test. Probably she lived in dread of that: there weren't any tests when *she* drove her first bullnose Morris, he could bet on it. And how could she and batty brother James get on, six miles from anywhere, without a car? There was no bus-service in Oldgrave, he knew, and if two old codgers were reduced to hiring a car, they could only afford it seldom.

'I'm sure you're years off eighty-seven, ma'am,' he said, and meant it, because her back was straight, her eyes were bright, and she talked sense. True, her face was a road-map of lines and she had that arthritic limp, but who wouldn't have lines, looking after a mindless old cove way up in his eighties, and quite young people could get arthritic hips, well anyway, people he would not like to call old.

His compassionate reflections upon old age were interrupted by a joyous cry from Mrs Peters. 'Oh, look, there he is, at the Church Corner. Oh, could you catch him for me before he oozes away somewhere else? I've walked *miles*.'

Up at the Church Corner, smiling down over the market place, was a very tall upright man who, from a distance, could be forty-five. And when the swift-moving policeman reached him, James Holly still looked forty-five. His hat concealed nearly all his pate, but there was some hair fringed round it. He was clean-shaven and had no lines on his face except the smile-lines.

'Mr Holly?' said the young bobby.

Total lack of response. Was the old boy deaf?

'Mr Holly?' much louder.

Dawning comprehension in the blank blue eyes. 'Jimmy Holly all present and correct,' said the tall man. 'You needn't shout, I'm not deaf.'

'Your sister has been looking for you, sir.' (Nutter or not, this chap rated a Sir. He and his sister, especially his sister, were the stuff.)

'God,' said Holly, 'can I never escape from sisters? Seven I have. Look after all their incomes, marriages, divorces, alimonies, funerals. How I hate sisters!'

'Your sister Mrs Peters thinks you may have mistaken the place where she parked her car, and it's time to be going home.'

'Nonsense,' said Jimmy Holly, 'little Janey, she's just married that ass Peters, she's far too young to be trusted with a car. And what do you mean by getting home?'

'You live with Mrs Peters at Fen Lodge, Oldgrave, sir.'

'I could never live in the same house as that ass Peters. What on earth are you talking about?' Jimmy, hitherto amiable, showed signs of affront.

But by this time the much slower dot-and-carry gait of Mrs Peters had brought her to the spot.

'Oh, *thank* you, officer,' she said wholeheartedly, 'we'll be all right now. Come along, Jimmy.'

She took the tall man's arm and without a word he turned to go with her. The young policeman watched for quite a while, until he saw them take the turning for the Chapel Street car-park.

'She's got something, that one,' he said to himself. 'Golly, it must be awful to be old and trying to cope with someone much older and dotty into the bargain. What can their home life be?'

Himself, he was recently married though he could barely afford it, and his home life was one jolly joke. There were no glasses among their wedding-presents, but lots of mugs – one of the penalties of living in an area self-conscious about its arty local potteries – so mugs had to do for every kind of drink. Well, they'd do, why not? A mug of beer, a mug of tea or coffee, a mug of rosé when friends came in, nothing wrong with mugs. They did have the good-housekeeping essential, a fridge, but no guarantee that in a thunderstorm their electricity would not fail. When it did, they managed with candles, a prayer that the fridge might not melt, and laughter.

But there could be precious little laughter for that harried, pretty, lame old girl with her ghastly slow-motion brother; nothing but the helpless sadness of old age with tragedy round the corner.

Back at the Station he said to a mate who had been longer in the town, 'Do you know a brother and sister from Oldgrave, he's batting steadily for his century but she probably won't stay with him though she's younger – ?'

'I know 'em. He'll last for ever, they do when their wits are gone. That's the brain that wears you out, bor. She's a good girl. I don't know how old, I've never had to ask, never caught her parked on a double yellow line yet. Mind you, she'd better not. Any trouble, and it's a driving test. Properly puts the wind up the old 'uns, a driving test.'

'I don't doubt it, a lot of bloody fuss about details when you've been driving OK for fifty years,' said the young bobby.

'More'n that, for your girl-friend,' said his mate, 'and not a smidgen on her licence. That I do know because one of our chaps, a new boy like you, got *him* going the wrong way in a one-way street in *her* car, which he'd pinched when she had 'flu. A proper balls-up. He never understood one word, he had no licence we could endorse and no money to pay a fine with. She was the one who came to Court, poor duck, and I wished the case had never been brought. We ought to've let the whole thing drop.'

'Didn't anyone on the Bench suggest that the brother ought to be shut up because she couldn't control him? I mean, it's obvious.'

'Everyone on the Bench had been friends with them for years, they knew she'd never hand him over to any kind of nut-house. She promised he'd never drive a car again and as far as I know he hasn't; I reckon the whole village keeps its cars locked since the case came up.'

'But she still can't manage him. Worn out she was, running up and down the streets and popping in and out of shops. Like a wagtail raising a cuckoo,' said the young policeman, who was a country boy, as were most of the others at the local nick; and in this small town no one was more than about half a mile from the country in any direction.

The young policeman could see in his mind's eye a little bird slim to emaciation dancing and darting around his parents' front lawn to catch gnats which she fed into the huge yellow mouth of a great fat chick sitting heavily on its rump and fluttering its rudimentary wings. He had often wondered if the wagtail foster-mother survived the strain of feeding that massive child of which she was so proud.

And he wondered now if pretty little lame old Mrs Peters would survive the strain of coping with big smiling idiot Jimmy Holly.

'D'you think that's family affection, keeps her running after that old brother?' he asked his longer-experienced mate.

'No, pride. Long after affection's been worn out, there's still pride. Come to think of it, none on us amounts to much without a bit of pride.'

'Costs you, though, pride does.'

'Tell me what doesn't cost you, bor, these days!'

Returned rather tired to her Oldgrave white elephant of a house, with brother safely in tow, Mrs Peters found she had a visitor: not unexpected: this was Maria Bowater's day, and but for time spent running around the Radmere streets after Jimmy, Jane would have been at home to welcome her old friend from Deanery House. This was the day when the Deanery House car conveyed those of its old residents who were fit and able, to visit for an hour or so their friends in the neighbourhood.

Janey told Maria, laughingly, about the chase round Radmere.

'Oh, my dear, that on top of everything else,' said old Maria. 'I can't think how you manage.'

'I do have a little house-help, you know. I just haven't the muscles now to handle the bedclothes. But kind Mrs Self up the Back Road, she does the heavy washing. Sheets, and Jimmy's long-johns, such very long johns: she's still young enough to have the strength for the job. And she can use the money, of course, but that's not the main thing – she's a kind woman and she knows what it's like.'

'Well, I'm glad you have that much help. But this great barn of a house, Janey.'

'He likes a big house, and when we came here he knew to the last penny what we could afford.'

'That was thirty years ago.'

'You're telling me! He doesn't know *now*. But I can't cut him down, Maria.'

'He's not your husband, you haven't made public promises to cherish him and all that.'

'I never had a chance to cherish my husband, he was shot down ten days after we married.'

'And you feel the need to cherish somebody?'

'Not only that. Jimmy looked after us all. We are nearly all dead now and Jimmy is well up in his eighties; I'm the only one who can say a thank-you for his care of us. Seven sisters. He never married, because four of his sisters couldn't be got rid of. He didn't get rid of *me* for long. My dear fighter-pilot hadn't any money to leave me. We all, the less lucky ones, looked to Jimmy and he managed well for us: he was darn' clever on the money-market. And look at him now!'

'You make me feel a coward, Janey, for taking refuge in Deanery House when really, with George gone, I could manage on my own. You're run off your feet and I'm totally lazy. You've not thought of putting Jimmy into some sort of home? Deanery House might not be able to take him – '

'Because he's nuts.'

'If you put it that way. But there's the Leathen Nursing Home, or really he wouldn't know the difference if he was in the geriatric ward at Castle Eyot. That's a very good one and somehow or other they have lots of nurses. Why don't you consider it?'

'This is his house,' said Janey Peters. 'I live here on his money so I have a duty to him. I've very little of my own, though I think I'll get a bit when Jimmy goes.'

'And by God you'll have earned it,' said Maria Bowater, relict of George, 'if you don't go first. Do look after yourself, Janey.'

'Oh, I do. What would Jimmy do without me?' said Jane Peters.

She was rather relieved when the Deanery House car pulled up at the gate to remove her friend Maria Bowater. People were always at her to get Jimmy *put away*. Like having a dear old dog *put down*. A geriatric ward or a well-chosen bin wasn't exactly death, but as near as made no difference. There were days when Jimmy, always happy, managed to be useful as well, looking after his greenhouse. The nights were the problem. Jimmy knew no difference between night and day: he would sleep all afternoon if he felt like it, and walk about most of the night. Their kind friend the doctor gave Jimmy sleeping-pills which didn't work, and Janey sleeping-pills which she did not take for fear of what Jimmy might get up to in the middle of the night. Once he set one of the rooms on fire but not disastrously because wakeful Janey smelt the smoke. No fire-engines, no publicity, no policemen, no injury, no doctor, just Janey with a fire-extinguisher and a wet blanket. So on that occasion no one said Jimmy ought to be confined in a geriatric ward or a bin. But it could happen again, it could be worse, impossible to hide. So Janey had wakeful nights and was too busy with housekeeping, cooking and shopping to catch up with her sleep in the daytime.

It was a blessing, though a minor one, that Jimmy was a gardener. On fine days he was happy weeding, planting, hoeing, and on the many days of rain, frost, snow, excluding even the best gardeners from their gardens, he pottered for hours in the greenhouse.

Fen Lodge was a big old house re-fronted in Georgian days, handsome, roomy, with a garden of nearly an acre; it stood high enough to overlook the 'fen', wet and reedy, of the upper waters of the river Doverey. In the short village street, the other houses were either older and smaller or newer and smaller. It was the big house of the street. That was why Jimmy Holly had fancied it. He thought big, in the days when he was capable of thinking at all. And he had a right to.

In those days, a man-of-all-work did the heavy in the garden and looked after the coke boiler and the car: cleaned the shoes and lived above the stables; while two young maids gave Jane some help and much amusing and instructive company. Jane learned how village life was lived by the cottage people; Jimmy never did.

But all these years later, there was no man-of-all-work because any man with any skill, or even without, could earn far more money than Jimmy, even in his full wits, would dream of paying, nor were there any little maids, for the same reason. The value of work had risen astronomically, the value of money had plummeted like lead. So Jimmy let the garden rampage more than somewhat but even now retained a link of reason and sympathy with his greenhouse plants – they were the cause of some of his midnight wanderings – while Jane had systematically reduced the house-cleaning to the irreducible minimum.

Cutting down in one way might mean more expenditure in another. For instance, without a man-of-all-work, a garage-hand had to be paid for changing a flat wheel – Jane simply had not the muscle, at her age, for any heavy job, and Jimmy had always, all his life, avoided anything which

L.F.—B

17

looked like hard slog, so he did not even know what to do. Fiddling round with pot-plants was Jimmy's 'work', and it was matter for thankfulness that he still did it.

He had forgotten everything he had ever known about business matters. Poor Jane had to lash her brains to income-tax and surtax papers, and hers were not the right sort of brains, so she had to keep the car on the road to go to Radmere to see bank-manager and accountant.

The bank charged on overdraft and the accountant charged anyway: these items of expenditure did not seem to make Jimmy Holly and Jane Peters any better off. However, if, Jimmy being lunatic and Jane inexperienced, they had simply paid out on every tax demand, they might have been worse off.

In 1975 they were far from rich, though when they bought Fen Lodge thirty years before, they had seemed rich: to some in the village a new invasion by the Affluent Society. But by the time the young policeman was hunting Jimmy round the town, the brother and sister were just poor old bods trying to get along in their too-big house because a move might be even more expensive. Nobody in Oldgrave thought them rich any more. Oldgrave people are mostly country working people with a realistic idea of the relative values of money and work. When Jimmy and his sister first arrived they were regarded with dark suspicion as city people who had a load of ill-gotten gains. But half a lifetime later it was clear that however ill-gotten their gains, they had not much left. They had not been loved when they were rich, but they became, as their circumstances narrowed, loved and cherished; part of the landscape.

2
Harold and Harriet

On the most minor road (there are three: this is the narrowest and most given to S-bends) between Oldgrave and the market-town of Radmere, a road without any public transport, naturally, public transport always trying to catch the most customers, not those in greatest need, stands Colham Hall, the home of a very ancient ex-farmer, Harold Brandling, and his only slightly less ancient wife Harriet. The wife meets Janey Peters when shopping, and would be a friend if she had time to make friends. She has exactly the same problem as Janey about her car, for Harriet is trotting along to eighty and her husband is eighty-five. At the slightest infringement, these damaging facts would come to light, and then what? Life in isolation, nourishment supplied by milkman, baker and Co-op van: the Brandlings were three miles from a shop, so their position would be worse than Janey's, who was at least in a village with two shops, a post office and a pub.

When Harriet looked around the extensive district served by the market-town, she never failed to be surprised and depressed by the number of very old people in all walks of life, those she knew personally and those she did not. Remarkably good air in East Anglia; we live for ever, she often remarked, in no congratulatory manner.

Some years before, the Brandling son, a young man in his forties who lived in a more habitable house on the Brandling acres, had taken over the running of the farms, but the old man still sat in his own office and did sums, seldom correctly because he could not accustom himself to having nothing between pounds and pees.

When the son became impatient about this, Harriet told him, 'You wait: this is only the first of the con-tricks. You wait till there are hectares instead of acres and kilos instead of tons and hundredweights, and you'll be foxed yourself.'

And gradually it came to pass; litres for pints, metres for yards, fabulous numbers of grammes for pounds, and always the customer getting a little less of whatever, for a little more money.

'They don't even get it *right*,' she complained. 'Who ever heard of Frenchmen talk about "kill-*omm*iters"? If we're supposed to be going Frenchified (search me why) we could at least try to appear literate.'

'But we aren't,' said her son, who was. 'We do the same thing with English, "con-*trov*ersy", putting the accent on the bit which means nothing. And you shouldn't let these little things worry you. There's a lot worse you can foam at the mouth about.'

'Don't I know it? Battery hens, battery calves, aerial crop-spraying with liquids, in your department, love: shipping helpless live animals for slaughter half a world away when they might just as well be exported as carcases and save all the terror. I'd be glad to leave this filthy world if

I was sure there was someone young to replace me. And I don't mean you, because your heart is in the right place but your pocket isn't, and a man with a family lives on his pocket, no one can get away from that.'

'You married into the wrong industry, Mum,' grinned her son.

'I didn't marry into an industry, I married – for love of your poor old father, I may tell you – into a way of life. It wasn't either so brutal then, or so liable to offer a choice between massive profits and bankruptcy. There was a nice, healthy, reasonably remunerative middle way. We survived, Daddy and I, you and your sisters. You were all educated well enough though not at huge expense. Nobody now is content with a middle way, it's millions or bust. It's not my way. I've always managed to earn enough, and it's better than too much.'

For Harriet was a well-qualified writer of studies, both learned and – occasionally – popular, of rural life, from the earliest records onwards. Her own pursuit of exact expression was what made her querulous about the slaughter of the language, not only by the Media but by those who were employed to teach it.

It was her heart, however, which made her fight for underdogs, mostly real animal underdogs because they could not utter for themselves. She was out of place as the wife of a farmer, and had been for well over fifty years, but during the Great Depression, which lasted in farming from 1924 to 1942, the Brandling acres could hardly have survived intact without her practical help. Those had been her great days, starting in the thirties: a modest fame for Harriet, but far more vitally, money to put into the Brandling farms for the ultimate benefit of the Brandling children.

In her old age, reputation and income dwindling as younger writers came into the field in competition, Harriet wrote more slowly and had time and heart to devote to the public good as she saw it. When she was not bemused by planning and executing a book, she wrote copious letters to the Press, regional and national, and was but seldom printed because she was no longer a top-line name. This she understood; it was about forty years since she had been a top-line name. But if she did not keep trying, why was she still alive? To keep her poor old moidered husband alive? Not an inspiring objective.

But he, in his pathetic old age, had become easy to live with. This had not always been so. When the children were young, male animal jealousy had made constant friction between Harold and Harriet. And in their long, long years together there had been times of financial stress, mostly Harold's, since Harriet was neither proud nor ambitious.

Harold's overdraft during the twenty bad years had been more than Harriet at her most productive could cope with. She wrote and wrote, but learned magazines did not pay well and publishers of books said that too-rapid production would look like pot-boiling and would become suspect among Harriet's highly specialized critics. Harold was a problem. He kept buying land and never sold any. Land looked cheap then, but you had to *do* something with it. 'Land-hungry' was Harold's middle name.

He scraped through. By 1942, the Second World War was paying out in gold.

Harriet had never stopped helping, because though Love had gone for a Burton the children were Harold's as well as hers. And all these years after, the children married and gone, Harriet and Harold living in a far-too-big house with a vast garden, the two of them small as mice in Paradise, they were kind and loving to each other as never before, united by – dogs and cats.

The beloved English Springer dog who had been child

after the human children left had been helped to die when old age seemed to be leading to pain. But there were still cats.

Forty years before, Harold had spat on cats. A shooting-dog was the only 'pet' for a farmer, and not much of a pet at that: chained to a kennel most of its life and fed once a day. Only two years after marriage, the non-life of the then pet spaniel had let to a shouting row.

'He loves you, God knows why,' yelled Harriet; 'why can't you love him? He isn't a lump of wood. He has affections, same like me, though mine are rapidly running out, I don't mind telling you. My affections were misplaced, like poor Jock's. You have nothing to give in return. Why the bloody hell should Jock and I love you if you don't love us?'

This led to regular walks for Jock the spaniel, simply because Harold was not quick-witted enough to find a basis for counter-attack. In the next fifty-odd years, he never found a basis for counter-attack. And now, in 1975, he didn't need one. No attack, no riposte called for. Harold and Harriet were at peace together, looking after cats.

There was very old neuter marmalade Sandy, neurotic, jealous, devoted to his human parents but not so far as to trust them. They kept letting Other Cats into the house. Sandy could not know that the Other Cats made a concerted rush round the ankles of whichever old person opened any door. Sandy did not wait to see, he took off to the top attic at the west end of the long, long, three-storey house, where there was a hole into the rafters. And there, if he were severely affronted, he would stay for days without food or drink. He was sixteen. He had been a kitten when the last dear dog was a puppy, and he had outlasted the dog by being thoroughly selfish. He spent his nights tucked closely under Harriet's chin. Not her idea of comfort, but his, and who, after sixteen years, could make him suffer rejection? Luckily Harriet did not also have a husband in her bed. They had had separate though communicating rooms ever since, forty years ago, Harold had had a traumatic episode with a burst appendix which had turned him into a bad sleeper. Harriet, naturally a good one, felt she could not do her manifold duties after nights with someone who heaved and scratched and moaned and groaned: and there were many bedrooms in the house. But now she had Sandy, who heaved and scratched and got up for loud slurping drinks of water three times in the night. Her day's work, however, was lighter. No children, and just as little cooking and cleaning as she cared to do. No one would complain.

Harold, too, loved Sandy, and Sandy loved Harold when Harriet was not available. The little furry arms would go round Harold's neck and the blunt gentle face be thrust against Harold's cheek. Had there been a time when he regarded cats as farm-animals which had to earn their keep by catching meece, no food provided except skim milk? Harold was good about Other Cats too: these simply arrived for food, having been informed by the feline bush tele-graph. And some of them were darlings, and too many of them stayed to have kittens and were then killed on the road which ran closely behind the house. Harold and Harriet were known as a source of kittens, but they did not part with kittens to just anybody.

Harriet never reminded Harold that once upon a time he'd have drowned the lot; no good raking up a past best for-gotten. Done is done. Stone-dead hath no fellow. She some-times said, 'It makes me laugh to remember how we damn' nigh slew ourselves to bring up our human children, and here we are, still bringing up children, four-footers, sweeties, prettier really than our own.'

'Less trouble and less cost, too.'

'At present prices, *not* less cost. What I pay for cat-food would have fed our children, when *they* were kittens, jolly well. As to trouble, at least we don't have to face an inquest when one of them gets killed on the road.'

'They give us more pleasure.'

'God, yes. Animals are so pleased with what we give them – they purr. None of our kids ever purred. Remember dear old Daniel's wagging stump of a tail? They spoil us, Harry. We are gods and we exploit them. It's a shame really.'

'But if we didn't look after these stray cats they'd all be dead on the road, and if a lot of people gave up keeping dogs, there'd be those many more rejected dogs to be put down by the police.'

'I only mean we do, without any justification, look on our animals as second-class citizens.'

'Sez you,' said old Harold. 'That Sandy, he's the lord of creation, he has you on a string. He's the top-class citizen in this house.' Not a hint of jealousy or malice, just a joke. Harold had certainly mellowed with age.

The fluctuating family of cats and the fond memory of the last devoted dog were the sweeteners in the life of the two old people. Without the animals there could have been acrimony, for Harriet was old, tired and overworked, while Harold was old, idle and increasingly vague.

They had grandchildren whom they did not forget – the son's family lived too near to be forgotten, even had the grandparents wanted to forget a good, bright trio, which they didn't.

Very far away there was an elder daughter married to an American with a bit of Army pension, farming in a fertile fold of desert where customers waited at the gate for free-range eggs, farm butter, veges grown without chemicals, and everlastingly the ranchmen for cattle-fodder because they could not be bothered to grow their own. There were no American grandchildren, but cats and a dog with whom

Harriet was in contact by post. Daughter Lydia in maturity resembled her mother in many ways.

Nearer home there was younger daughter Meg, much harried and 'sair hodden doon' by parenthood but still a great slogger at ball-games, and something else too which allied her to her mother – a painter. The daughters both had much of Harriet incorporated in their natures. The son was Harold over again, nervy, short-tempered, manic about money, cursed with ulcers, a despiser of women. But if he ever reached eighty he too might be a lover of cats and dogs: there was this link with his mother which had so unexpectedly turned out to connect with his father too. Maybe in old age, animals offered the adoration which human relatives no longer supplied, if ever they had.

The outstanding difference between Harold and Jonathan was that Jonathan understood pounds and pees and Harold never would.

Harriet chatted to her part-time helper and to many people in the town when she went shopping – how could one know what was on, without chatting? Almost every day of the week she had to go into town because Harold had nothing else to do until the afternoon television came on. (He could not listen to radio much because of the demand it made on the imagination to fill in the faces and the scenery. He had never had any imagination.)

Not many of the people to whom Harriet chatted had the impertinence to say outright that it was absurd for two old things to occupy a house which would be listed by any agent mad enough to entertain the idea of selling it as containing 4 sit. 11 bed, 2 bath, c.h., large kit., scullery, larder and butler's pantry. But they all thought so, and so did Harriet, and heartily agreed. She knew besides that the roof leaked disastrously in three places and that the second bathroom, a late addition, produced only boiling water and no cold.

The C.H. was temperamental in the extreme, and it would be wise of any agent to keep silent about the water-supply and drainage. As with public transport, the other public services avoided an area of such sparse rateability.

Electricity, however, had come in World War Two because of the farms, and worked well enough except that in those dark and ignorant days nobody, certainly not Harold, stood out for enough light and power points in a house. Harold had been thinking of money, as usual; the house ran a bad second to the farms.

Harriet was heartily sick of a too-large house in which nothing worked properly. The sash-cords of the eighteenth-century front windows were always broken, the lav-chains seldom achieved what one expected, the leaking roof inhibited any ambitions towards indoor redecoration, and in thunderstorms the strictly local transformer was always struck and the light and power failed in the house as well as on the farms. No one cared a dime about the house, as long as the milking machines on Top Farm could be switched on to the private motor generator and made to function somehow.

Harriet, in spite of having given most of her life to the awkwardly large house, also all the people, including at one period three servants, who lived in it, *and* to the huge garden, felt she could easily curb her untidiness (which had grown, by Parkinson's Law, to fill the space available) and could live in a caravan with her typewriter and the cat Sandy. But Harold, so old, so rooted in the past, so pathetic, had achieved the prime ambition of his life, to live in the big house of the parish in which he had been born. He wouldn't move until six strong men carried him out in a coffin. And because of promises made in church before witnesses fifty-six years before, Harriet, for very pride, would stay with him.

What if he were to become incontinent, bedridden, beyond the care of an old woman nearly eighty? The geriatric ward? Harriet pushed this all-too-obvious probability out of her mind. He *might* have a stroke or a heart-failure and simply die suddenly and almost without pain in the surroundings which he deemed suitable, the big old house and the huge garden whose deficiencies did not bother him and on the ownership of which he was frequently complimented. He looked, by his own choice, like a down-at-heel tramp, and smelt accordingly, but everyone knew he was the big man in the big house of Colham village, and Harriet hoped he would not have to suffer a come-down before the end. It would be especially awful for Harold, to become just another anonymous old thing in one of the several Old Folk's Homes or the geriatric ward.

The notion that she might be the one to go suddenly by stroke or heart-attack, leaving Harold in the lurch, did not occur to her. She had never yet left anyone in the lurch, however overworked or physically enfeebled she might be. An excessive conscientiousness, the thing which drove her to write letters to newspapers and often made her a bore to herself and others, was a near-lifelong reaction against parents who had conspicuously lacked it. At fifteen, she had found quite suddenly and without warning, at the end of a summer term, that she did not even know the respective addresses of her parents, nor, for that matter, any 'home' address for herself. From then on, she had resolved to resemble that irresponsible couple as little as she might. She knew about inherited genes but she also believed in acquired character.

A serious woman, Harriet, compelled by circumstances to be so, a woman who hoped to inculcate basic sense in her children, a woman lacking in tenderness, a highly educated and capable creature whose springs of warmth had been early checked, and dried up finally by Harold, whose need was sex, not sentiment.

But with a pen in her hand she was not boring to herself or anyone else. She was as concentratedly happy as ever her father had been with a gun in his hand, toiling over moors in pursuit of grouse or deer. Each to his taste, to each some taste, some fun, some happiness. (The trouble with Father had been that he had too many, too much and too often.)

The young policeman in the town, in collusion with the traffic warden, had his eye on Harriet as well as on Janey Peters, though Harriet did not look her age except first thing in the morning when she had to unscrew every screaming joint in order to get out of bed. There were hardly any mornings which looked like lovely days, however sweetly the sun sent fingers of light among the tree-shadows on the dew-silvered park at Colham Hall. But by ten-thirty a lovely day sometimes seemed possible.

Years ago, the first sunbeams were the ones laid on the page by a loving pen, as carefully as a painter might lay them on canvas with a brush. But that was years ago. Arthritic old women toddling along to eighty were not so enthusiastic about sunrise – they did not sleep so satisfyingly in the dark hours.

3
The Gaults and the Howletts

A few miles down-river (the Doverey hardly a river yet) there was once a lovely unspoiled village green, dominated at one end by one of those East Anglian junior-cathedrals and a huge rectory, and flanked along one side by a big old farmhouse, a pub and many farm cottages each in its bit of garden: the other side of the Green displaying a totally collapsed fifteenth-century thatched timber-and-plaster house with about four acres of run-to-seed land about it. Soon after the end of World War Two, Brigadier Gault (retd.) bought the wreck and two thistly acres with a few cankered apple-trees for next to nothing, and stripped the house of its plaster, exposing the studs and thereby making the house as cold as the grave. It looked beautiful. It proclaimed its great age.

But next to the Gault acres was the piece of rubbishy land which the Brigadier did not want, a couple more acres of weeds – the two he had acquired would keep him busy enough, turning them into a vegetable-garden. After some years, this nettlepatch was purchased by a person called Howlett, a retired shop-steward, at the opposite political pole from the Brigadier and no social buddy either. This Howlett built a red-brick bungalow and started on his great ambition, to turn the nettlepatch into a riot of colour. He was the perfect suburbanite, risen from the ranks of industrial terraced back-to-backs. Had he had the support of, say, fifteen other inhabitants of bungalows or chalets on an estate, the nettlepatch and near by, he could have accomplished something of social worth, such as improving the smelly darkness of the pub by the addition of a juke-box and a bandit. But on his own he was out of place in Willington Green. Fortunately he was far too busy on his big garden, for some time after he and his wife moved in, to realize this.

Years before the Howletts arrived on the nettlepatch, the Brigadier started his habit of rising when the birds awoke him – seven a.m. in winter but four in summer – and taking one of his guns, the double-barrel twelve bore or the little double-barrel four-ten, to shoot out of his bedroom window at those birds which threatened his vegetables. As his had been the only house on that side of the Green except the huge empty Rectory and the huge empty House of God, nobody complained, though the shots did waken Miss Weetch and others on the far side of the Green.

But Howlett, moving in the moment his bungalow had dried out, was another matter. Howlett, his wife Clara and his wife's pedigree Schnauzer were so near as to be awakened and kept awake by the Brigadier's shots; and long after the shooting had stopped, the Schnauzer, a town dog unused to sounds of battle at dawn, went on yapping neurotically, so the Howletts were not the only ones to suffer. The Brig had been accustomed to drop off to sleep again after his cock-light fusillade, but the Schnauzer would not let him.

The two men, though poles apart politically and socially, were not unalike in character. Whatever the Government was up to, the Brig, a choleric type, was agin it – though more frequently and furiously, of course, when the Government was Labour: while Howlett was a strong man in opposition to anyone who might be considered boss-class. Such as a senior Army officer (retd.).

Nor were their wives poles apart. Cowed Mrs Gault had always wanted a dog but had never been allowed to have one. Non-cowed Clara Howlett loved her dog as though it were her youngest child. Mrs Gault and Mrs Howlett had spoken about dogs over the garden fence on the very first day the Howletts moved in. These two women, one pathetically a gentlewoman and the other not yet altogether genteel, recognized one another instantly as sisters under the skin, born to be mothers and aunts of dogs. Especially dogs with hairy faces and devoted bright eyes, clear as sherry, peering through the thickets.

Irene Gault had not since childhood been able to learn much about dogs because her husband, whom she had married in her first London Season, thought of them only as possible aids to shooting; and as it happened, the ever-changing course of their Army life had prevented even this superficial acquaintance such as sportsmen have with their strictly outdoor dogs. Irene was dogless for life and also childless. The Brigadier blamed her, naturally, for failure to conceive, and at the relevant time it had dawned on only a few in the medical profession that a *man* could be sterile. Anyway, who then was brave enough to make the Brig undergo tests? And it was too late now. Irene Gault was unalterably childless, and dogless to boot.

Clara Howlett, on the other hand, had three grown-up

children, though she was ten years younger than Irene: children who worried her only a little: they had all their marbles and all their fingers and toes, so they were capable of going their respective ways without calling on her for help or advice. That was why she had her loving hairy Schnauzer, who did need her, because her husband was not really dog-minded, and now that the children were gone he was only interested in a riot of colour in his garden and the hope of joining an angling club. His wife was welcome to her nice hairy dog. She had to have something and she was not keen on fishing. Irascible Howlett was a more reasonable man than irascible Gault.

The first word the two wives had came from Irene, across the Howletts' brand-new fence. The Howletts' furniture was being moved in, and irascible Howlett as yet knew nothing of irascible Gault's early-morning gun-play. Clara Howlett had let the Schnauzer loose in the nettlepatch, to give him freedom after a long car-ride.

'Oh!' cried Irene Gault, shocked out of her shyness by sheer pleasure, 'what a darling dog: what kind is he?'

Clara told her, and told her too what an intelligent easily-trained chap Dog Peter was, and how loyal and loving. 'Don't you have a dog, Mrs – ?'

'Gault. Irene Gault. My husband doesn't like dogs, I'm afraid.' She was always afraid about something, and Clara Howlett guessed it.

'Oh, well, that's no good then. A dog knows. You'd get a difficult half-hearted dog if he knew his master wasn't on his side. I can't say my hubby knows a lot about them but he likes being loved by Peter and he lets me be Mother.'

'How lucky you are!'

Clara Howlett did not quite know how to interpret this but took it easy and said, 'You don't always get the perfect dog. It would be kind to take one from a Dogs' Home, but you never know how it's been treated by the people who dumped it there. I wanted a mongrel from a Home but my hubby advised against it, so we paid a lot for Peter as a pup. I still feel awful about those poor hopeful dogs in Homes.'

'Oh, don't,' begged Irene Gault. 'I can't bear to think of them, or cats either. I could keep a whole zoo here, but my husband the Brigadier – '

'Say no more. They're the bosses, damn' 'em,' said Clara Howlett. 'I don't have to damn mine all that often, but he's an awkward cuss, he needs understanding. If he hadn't have been awkward he'd never have held down his job – '

At that moment a loud hail from the new bungalow tore Clara away, so Irene, her dull life stirred out of its torpor, had to remain unsatisfied. But she knew enough of her Brig to realize that awkwardness could be a professional asset. Though it wasn't much of an asset in family or social life.

This pleasant interchange about dogs had taken place in October, a customary time for changing houses, and there was the winter to come, and the early spring, in which the Brigadier's war on winged predators was at a time when passing traffic dimmed the noise of his gunshots. It was not until the following May (meantime the Howlett garden was well on the way to its riot of colour) that irascible Howlett was awakened by Gault's gunshots in what seemed to him the small hours and was kept awake by the Schnauzer's hysteria, which also maddened irascible Gault.

Some men take pride in being irascible. They think it's – what? Impressive, frightening, a show of strength? Only fools are impressed, only cowards are frightened, and in the end it is seen as a show of weakness (if you can't be boss in any other way, lose your temper). Irascibility is mostly used in a very limited circle – husband and wife, husband, wife and young children – where the audience can be cowed. If the audience is not cowed, irascibility evokes contempt.

So what happens when two irascibles, Brigadier Gault and ex-shop-steward Howlett offend one another by (a) shooting off firearms at unsocial hours, and (b) keeping a yapping dog?

Behind the scenes the two wives grieved and offered each other piecemeal explanations.

'Peter's a town dog, he never heard a gun before. It's so sudden, before proper daylight. He thinks it's dangerous for us.'

'We have never had a dog, barking or otherwise. My husband, that's another thing, has always thought himself monarch of all he surveyed this side of the Green, but of course he isn't now and he doesn't understand.'

'They both just don't understand. Men!' said Clara Howlett. 'If there weren't any men there'd be a lot more peace and friendship and prosperity.'

'But there wouldn't be any children,' said Irene Gault. 'I never had any, but you did. Would you want to be without them, to be *dead* when you die?'

Clara Howlett hastily muttered something about not wanting to be without her kiddies of course, having nothing of comfort to offer to the other woman, who was not much alive while she lived and would certainly be totally dead when she died.

The incident which brought the young policeman to Willington Green was the shooting of Peter the dog by the Brigadier. All the dog received was a couple of pellets in the hinder parts, for the Brig was no great shot and the most he did to his foes the birds was to scare them; Peter, however, was a larger and less mobile target, and from the noise he made he might have been dying in agony.

Already there had been the usual fusillade at the birds which had alerted the dog to danger and set him off barking.

After half an hour during which the Brigadier had gone back to bed but the dog had not, Mrs Howlett let the dog out into the garden to see if freedom would pacify him. It did not; it brought him vociferously near the Gaults' bedroom window and the Brigadier leapt out of bed and shot him. Peter yelled like a banshee and tore home, carrying a hind leg. In less than a minute Clara Howlett was out, in curlers, the rather big dog in her arms, addressing the Brigadier in terms most unsuitable on the lips of one who was climbing into the Middle Class.

'You bloody old butcher, you've shot my dawg!'

The Brigadier thrust out of his window a rough-headed thin scarlet face on a long scrawny neck and bawled back, 'Why don't you keep the beast quiet, you fool woman?'

'It's you what starts it off with your sodding gun. What right have you to let off guns before it's properly daylight?'

'I can do what I like to protect my property from birds or any other trespassers, madam.'

Howlett, in far handsomer pyjamas than the Brigadier's, joined the party in time to hear this.

'That you can't,' he shouted. 'Your neighbours have the right to a night's sleep. Your bloody property's no more important than mine.'

'It's been here five hundred years.'

'Time it was gone, then. It 'ud burn a treat, all that timber 'n thatch. Any more trouble from you and you won't have a property, Lord Muck.'

So the Brigadier loosed off his gun at Howlett. It was fortunate that, especially when irate, he was a very bad shot.

The earth spattered up round Howlett, who rushed indoors while in the other house the Brigadier rushed downstairs, each to his telephone. The hour was not yet six a.m. The night duty officer at Radmere Police Station, in contact first with Howlett, wisely decided to write down as much of the affair as he could understand and pass the buck to the day-boys.

'You wish to bring a charge against Brigadier Gault?'

'You bet I do. He shot my wife's dog first then took a pot at me. He's dangerous. Ought to be locked up.'

'What kind of gun?'

'I wouldn't know, I don't use guns, but it peppered poor doggie's backside and I reckon I was lucky to escape.'

'Do you know *why* he was letting off his gun at that hour in the morning?'

'He always does, at first light, when the dickybirds start feeding on his veges. That's another thing: anyone popping off guns in the small hours is committing a nuisance, wouldn't you say? I mean there's a law regulating automatic bird-scarers, so why not human ones? It'll be four a.m. next month. How'd you like that, if it was you next door?'

'Right, sir,' said the night officer, feeling strongly that the appellant had grounds for complaint. 'I've set it all down, and you will be hearing from us as soon as the day shift comes on.'

'I'd bloody better, else I'll have to dig myself an air-raid shelter,' said Howlett and rang off.

Immediately the phone rang again.

'This is Brigadier Gault, speaking from Willington Green. I have been threatened by my neighbour, a man called Howlett – '

'How did he threaten you, sir?'

'To burn my house down. He said it would burn a treat – his expression, not mine – because it's timber and thatch. And if he carries out his threat it *will* burn a treat, ask any insurance company. I need police protection from him, Officer. And I wish to charge him in Court with threatening behaviour.'

Sergeant Ames felt his opinion swinging more than a little

between the compass-points of Howlett and Gault. Right on both sides, as so often, blast it.

'I have noted it all down, sir, and you will soon be visited by officers of the day shift,' he said.

'But damn it, I want police protection *now*, and until that incendiary lunatic is behind bars!' yelled the Brigadier, hurting poor Ames's ear.

'You can't have it now, sir, because there's only me at the Station pro tem.,' said Ames, 'nor you don't need it, that I can see: you're the one with the gun.'

'But my property is in danger!'

'And you put the other bloke in danger of his life by shooting at him, so I now heard. He was before you on the phone. Two of a kind I'd say,' concluded Ames, 'and if you're both still alive by mid-morning, you might both go on living.' He was just about up to the neck with his spell of nights. His two constables, running round in that silly white car with POLICE on it, advertising their presence, had the easy time; he, stuck in the Station because he was near retirement and it didn't matter if he got disgruntled, had all the funny stuff, most of it mere nothings, to deal with: husbands who hadn't come home to bed, dogs and even cats who hadn't come home to bed: broken-down cars needing directions to all-night garages: you name it, if it was boring enough Ames had it. But this one was different: it had roused some feeling in Ames; he'd have to think about it when he went off duty. Both those ruddy idiots who ought to've known better had got him angry.

About ten in the morning a police car driven by the youngest constable and containing the day sergeant (called Thomas) drew up on Willington Green, strictly midway between the two paths-of-access, one to Thatchers, the other to Howlett's bungalow which had no name as yet. A man hastened out of each house. The two of them started a shouting-match beside the car but the sergeant took no notice at all until a brief pause occurred, when he said, 'The Station's the right place for you two *gentlemen* to be saying all that. Get in, please.'

Meanwhile the young driver had been observing something else. At the Station, after the contestants had made their statements, to the secret amusement of the shorthand-writer, and had been taken home again, he told Sergeant Thomas, 'D'you know, Sarge, the two women, the wives of them turkey-cocks, were sitting together on the old military buster's lawn, bathing the backside of the poor doggie, and the doggie was looking up into their faces and never letting out a squeak. All happy together. Makes you think.'

'What does it make you think?'

'That most men are nutters and most women are the sane ones. I've often thought that, Sarge.'

'Don't you get thinking too much, bor. We go by the book. Facts, not thinking.'

'That's a fact, them two wives aren't in this damn' silly upset.'

'You wait, laddie, and some day you'll see the female of the species doing her stuff. Don't get large-sized general notions: keep down to the facts.'

During the absence of the two plaintiff-defendants at the Police Station, the vet had come to see poor Peter – neither of the wives could drive a car, neither had ever been allowed to try – and had easily removed two number-six-shot pellets from the dog's hind-quarters. Peter's sad, puzzled expression was scarcely lightened, but he was jumping about on all four legs and asking to go for a walk on the Green. He, the most injured, was the least affected by the feud.

Which was not ended yet. After the so-called 'reorganiza-tion', which most of the suffering public called disorganization, of all Local Government functions, the magistrates sat less often, so that there was a time-lag of more than a month before the foaming contestants, still passionately determined, could put their respective cases to the Authority to which the police were equally determined to bring them. Both defendants (as they now were) disdained the aid of lawyers. Neither doubted his own ability to do better than any hired word-merchant.

It was in fact Police-Sergeant Thomas who outlined the case, bringing witnesses from the Green to testify to the Brigadier's early-morning habits. After which all the old stuff poured out from Howlett and the Brigadier.

'He shot my dog and took a pot at *me*, I ask you! He's dangerous!'

'He threatened to burn down my house. I need protection from him!'

To Howlett the Chairman said, 'Is the dog dead?'

'Well, no, but he has two holes in his backside, poor chap.' (Laughter in Court, quickly suppressed.)

'And did you suffer any damage yourself?'

'Well, no, but it was *meant*.'

'That you cannot know. Attempted murder? That's hard to believe.'

'You lot are all friends of his, that's why you don't believe it.'

'I didn't hear that, nor did you, Sergeant.'

To the Brigadier: 'When you fired at your neighbour did you mean to kill him?'

The Brigadier said in a strained voice unlike his own, because he found lying difficult, 'No, only to frighten him.'

'But you hoped to kill his dog?'

'It yapped for hours on end and it's only a dog.'

(Sensation, as in any British Court).

'But, Brigadier, as I understand it you were the cause of the yapping. You were the one who wakened the neighbours up, and not only the Howletts, at peep of day with your shooting. The dog, coming from a city, where only criminals shoot, was naturally alarmed.'

'Yapping brute. Kept everyone awake.'

'But not until you had already awakened everyone,' the Chairman pointed out.

The magistrates then retired.

In their nasty little back room the woman magistrate said forcefully, 'They ought to be allowed to get on with it. No loss to the community if they put an end to each other.'

'Fine,' said a quiet little grey Beak with a twinkle, 'if it stopped there. But there's the dog. And I believe they both have wives.'

'Were the wives in Court?'

'I think not. No good as evidence anyway, wives, and I gathered from the sergeant that the quarrel was none of theirs.'

Having spent but little time in deliberation, the Bench filed back and the Chairman told the assembly that in this kind of squabble (he clearly enjoyed this diminishing term) between neighbours, criminal charges seemed absurd; so both parties would be bound over, each in the sum of two hundred pounds, for two years. And if either party thought the sum excessive, let him consider the threats which had been made and the actual injury inflicted, if only upon a dog. There must be no more noisy bird-scaring except during the hours when farmers were allowed to use mechanical scarers, and no more physical damage to any person or any person's pet animal, nor any more threats to burn anybody's house down: was that clear?

To both parties two hundred pounds was at that juncture an awful lot of money. To the Brigadier because he was never quite out of the red, and to Howlett because he was paying for his bungalow. Both left the Court chastened, possibly ashamed because in summary it all sounded so silly; but very far from reconciliation.

4
People, Various

The Gault-Howlett case made a half-column in the county daily, but rated a banner headline and much more detailed reporting in the strictly local weeklies. The Howletts were not yet well known in the Radmere catchment area, hardly even in Willington Green, since it takes a Suffolker years to know anybody well: but the Gaults were known even outside their village by gentles and simples alike because their residence had been long enough to be called 'living' and the Brigadier had made his mark. The locals for some distance around Radmere read avidly (having already heard a good deal by word of mouth long before the Court case) the statements of police and protagonists and the Chairman's denigrating remarks.

In their own village the pub had a field-day. It was a true pub, old, darkish, uncomfortable but friendly, its sole non-liquid entertainment a dart-board. Consequently it was no place either for the Brigadier, who was not a mixer, nor for Howlett who was used to modern plastic-and-chromium pubs with 'music'. The true locals at their local could let themselves go.

'Serves th' owd barstud roight,' said Pensioner Joe Fludd from across the Green. 'Wake us up afore cock-light he do. Buds is a pest in a gardin, all on us knows, but *we* dassn't loose orf guns at 'em in ungodly hours so whoy should he?'

'Becorse he's a Brigadier, Lord o' Creation,' explained with heavy irony Bill Colley, farm-worker. 'He ain't loike us.'

'Sez he, but owd Sam Jiggens on the Bench say different,' said Joe Fludd. 'Cut him down proper he did.'

'Would you say,' inquired an elderly man in spectacles, 'that you loike that new feller Howlett any better?'

'We don't know nawthen, to really know, about neether one on 'em,' said a very old codger, bald as a coot, bright as a button. 'Not same as we know Mr Warden, let's say, what's been farmin' here all his loife and his father and gran-fer before him. That-air Howlett's *new*, and the Brigadier hain't been in Willington Green more'n thutty year.'

'And what's thutty year?' jeered a young fellow of perhaps twenty-two, a truck-driver.

'A nawthen, same as you, bor,' said the bald sage. 'That take a loifetoime to git to know a man, and all the better do yar dad and grandad knowed *his*. I'd trust moy loife to John Warden, but not to these here new buggers, neether on 'em, nor yet to you, Charlie Knott.'

'You're roight there, anyways, Uncle,' said the young chap, with a grin as Satanic as his pleasant features could contrive. Everyone knew he had expectations from his bachelor uncle the sage, so those within earshot roared and the nearest punched the lad on the shoulders. But the dominant topic, the Court case, was not allowed to lapse.

'Whoy din't they take owd Brig's gun-licence away? He ain't safe with a gun,' asked someone from a corner.

'Becorse he's a pal of all them on the Bench,' said Bill Colley. 'You or me'd have lorst our licences do we had any, but not him.'

'Next toime he shoot a dawg or a cat or a 'uman bean, let all on us git up a Round Robin to hev him put in a bin,' suggested the man in the corner.

'That's comin' it a bit strong,' said the sage. 'He hev a sharp temper and his notions don't mix with the present day. But you'll all be sayin' the same about me 'fore long.'

'Non-sense, Uncle!' cried the young truck-driver, making two stresses in the word and thus giving it more meaning. Suffolkers often say non-sense, no sliding over it.

'Well, thank you kindly, booy,' said the sage, 'but that's as may be, dependin' on how long the Brig and me manage to goo on livin'. Ideas change. Five year, ten year, and the bloke what was a one-time hero is a devil and the devil is a hero. We hev to live and think our thoughts and do our best, we hain't got no mastery of anything but our own selves. And you not even that, Charlie bor, the way you bump around these-here narrer lanes just becorse fifty moile an hour is permitted by law.'

Charlie said, 'Whoy not other droivers look out fer me? I'm doin' a job o' work, them in their cars is doddlin' orf to cocktail parties.'

'Come a head-on, who's dead?' said his uncle. 'Not you, up there in yar cab loike in a tank. The other feller down there loike a squashed beetle. You and yar droivin' put me in moind of the Brig and his gun; Lord of Creation stuff. But we ain't none on us, not one, Lord of Creation.'

Charlie did not defend himself. He had a great respect for his uncle who was reputed to have nearly a thousand quid to leave. Even if it was only a couple of hundred it would be worth having.

The last word on the Gault-Howlett topic in the pub that night was said by the sage: 'Pity th' owd booy's woife's sech a pore fule. What are females for but to put a bit o' sense in men?'

Charlie mumbled so no one could hear, 'You was never married, so maybe all the stuff you dish out ain't such good sense arter all.' He felt all wrong saying this, even to himself, but he was rattled by his uncle's criticism of his driving. His licence, which he had had for three years, was his pride and joy. He could drive anything, however huge, and he had never hit anything large enough to cause him to feel a bump. (It was other people, not the truck-drivers, who knew about the road-harvest of cats, young rabbits, leverets, hedgehogs, even birds – skittering partridges with their bee-like chicks, and overfed hand-reared pheasants.)

Farther along the same side of the Green was the one Willington shop-of-all-sorts. Mr and Mrs Potts seldom went to the pub; they took stock, did accounts (their sub-post office made extra work) and watched television in the evenings. But they took time off in their sitting-room to discuss the Gault-Howlett affair more freely than they could with their gossipy customers. The two wives in the case were also customers.

'That poor little Mrs Gault, I'm sorry for her. She'd never be one to get across her neighbours,' said Mrs Potts. 'Couldn't say Boo to a goose.'

'And that's a pity. She's got a goose who badly needs being said Boo to,' said Mr Potts. 'I'm thankful that Howlett, being new here and not yet intimidated by military rank and a bullying manner, has brought the Brig's goings-on into the public eye. I don't see why we should be driven to sleeping-pills in the hope of not being wakened at peep of day.'

'And anyway the pills have done most of their job by then, so we jump out of our skins just the same,' said Mrs Potts. 'Last June it was four a.m., that's when the birds start. It's daylight. I know because he woke me up regularly, and one can't get to sleep again.'

'It used to be the farmers and their automatic poppers, so we didn't notice him so much. But now the farmers are cut down by law. So why should God Almighty Gault think he's above the law?'

'Perhaps he doesn't, now,' said Mrs Potts, 'and it must be an awful shock to him to realize that he's no better than the rest of us.'

'Mind you, I'm not all that addicted to the man Howlett, the bloody Red,' said Potts. 'If he had his way there'd be no more small shopkeepers like us, making private profits, ha-ha, for ourselves, what we can keep out of the clutches of the Inland Revenue – '

'God help village people, then,' said his missis. 'Perhaps he'll learn. His wife's a nice woman, comes here a lot, can't get to Radmere often, where there's the Co-op, not only because of the price of petrol but because he won't let her learn to drive.'

'He could be wise. I'm often worried about you on the roads. And maybe Radmere wouldn't make him any happier: it's full of private enterprise. But if he stays here, his mind may broaden a bit.'

'He'll stay. He's doing wonders making a garden out of that old wilderness. When you start making something, you stay with it,' said Mrs Potts.

These two, now in their active fifties, had bought the village shop twenty years before for the sake of their two children, and they had never regretted leaving Birmingham. In the small village school (now closed) individual talent had been recognized. In the larger Radmere schools to which the children progressed, hooligans and vandals were very few, and a child's individual talent was still recognized, not swamped by sheer numbers or indiscipline. The Potts children did well enough at school and were now, in their twenties, making careers, far distant from their parents in mileage, but not out of touch. There was a postal service not only from the north of Scotland where Katie was matron cum cook in an Adventure Centre, but also from Canada where George was a teacher.

Mrs Potts often said, 'It's as much as we can expect: they're grown up, and they couldn't stick around *here*. But you can depend on it, love, if there was any trouble, theirs or ours, they'd be on our doorstep or we'd be on theirs quicker than *that*. Trouble's the real test.'

'Test of what?'

'The word's seldom spoken in families. Love.'

'We often call each other "love", you and I.'

'That's habit. A good habit, but we do it without thinking. *They* would think, when they came rushing to our help or sent for us to come to theirs. Though they probably wouldn't say.'

'I wonder how much love there is in the Brig's house?' said Mr Potts. 'D'you think they call each other "love"?'

'Heavens, no, it's vulgar and kind of dialect, mainly north-country. May deeah, he might call her if he was feeling amiable, if he ever feels amiable. But I wouldn't be surprised if the Howletts weren't quite a companionable couple, like us. He lets her keep a dog, and the dog likes him. You let me keep cats and the cats think you're the cats' pyjamas. It's a sort of indication of an OK household.'

'Never heard anything so daft,' said Mr Potts. 'We need the cats for the shop, for the mice – '

'But we don't need Thomasina sleeping between us in our bed, do we, *luv*?' said Mrs Potts. Thomasina was the youngest child of them both, just as Peter the Schnauzer was the youngest child of the Howletts.

'*You* don't chuck her out.'

'Nor do you. We both love Thomasina. Like we did, like we do our human kids.'

'OK, you win. There's a word, a clean word, which we avoid just as hard as we try to avoid the dirty ones. Or harder.'

'Definitely harder. Because it's embarrassing. The dirty ones are common currency now, like devalued pees. But the clean ones, they make people stare, like you were trying to get change for hundred-pound notes.'

At the Rectory at the next village southwards called Forde, the wife of the parson, whose cure of souls now included Willington Green (since the Church started hoarding its resources, having sensibly abandoned hope of free money from the faithful), read the local rag at breakfast and said to her husband who was a bit late as usual, 'Alan, what happens when an irresistible force meets an immovable object?'

'I've never really known. You're the scientist. But my guess is an almighty great explosion. Why?'

'You should watch out. I think this one was a bomb which didn't quite go off, but next time . . . Read this, Alan, and tell me which is the irresistible force and which the immovable object. They're both your parishioners.'

The Reverend read the account of the Court case. 'No doubt,' he said. 'Howlett is the irresistible force and the Brigadier the immovable object. Oh dear.'

From the Reverend Alan Dickin, 'Oh dear' was a swear-word. He had abjured all the others when first he put on his dog-collar.

He was a young man, as Rectors go; only in his thirties. His wife Helen was about the same age. Their two children bicycled to Primary School at Castle Eyot, which gave Helen the shudders because an important main road had to be crossed. Alan had faith in God, and if God let the children be killed, Alan would submit, but Helen wouldn't. She would simply curse God and die. The children had to bicycle because they were marginally outside the school-bus limit: so they could walk, bicycle or be taken in their daddy's or mummy's car like so many others in a similar situation. But the stipend did not run to a separate car for Mummy, and Daddy regarded his as dedicated to the work of his parishes – three all told – and the two children, bright and brave, longed to bicycle anyway. As for walking, if the grown-ups were in a lather about safety, walking was worse. They knew all about crossing the main road: they'd been taught at school in the infant days when Daddy or Mummy had been compelled to take them in the car. Apart from the main road, bicycling was a doddle.

But Helen, who sometimes drove the car for shopping when Alan was not using it, knew that nothing was a doddle. Along the narrowest of roads, huge lorries with bulky loads of stuff for farms came pounding. And even the drivers of ordinary saloon cars seemed to suppose, if they were young and had just passed their test, that the legal limit of 50 m.p.h. on these roads was a minimum, not a maximum, else why were their speedos calibrated up to 100?

If the Dickin children were killed on the road, Alan would say, 'The Lord gave and the Lord hath taken away. Blessèd be the name of the Lord,' but Helen would not bless the Lord or anybody else for giving and then taking away. People who give and then take away had better not give. A gift is a gift is a gift – if you believe that God sends the babies independently of the activities of Pa and Ma in bed.

Helen had much difficulty in putting on the face of a religious woman. Poor dear victimized Jesus Christ she could love because there was quite good evidence for much of his life and teaching, even allowing for the natural bias of Matthew, Mark, Luke and John. But the Father, the supposedly omnipotent God, creator of this mess the world, she could not take. No good discussing it with Alan, he'd swallowed the lot. It seemed to Helen that there were two distinct strains of religious belief, one social, based on the life and teaching of J.C., and the other anti-social, based on ignorant worship of something called God, having little to do with Jesus Christ. Everyone knew by 1975 that the world had not been created by anybody, which was a darn' good thing because nobody, not even a god, could be blamed for the foul-up. Everyone knew about the slow and chancy process of evolution on a vaguely circular lump of matter which had come together in the same way as the other occupants of Space. Aeons before there were men to dream up a god, there had been life – not human – on earth. Helen knew she ought not to have married a simple-minded parson, she a geologist and palaeontologist, but she had loved him and she loved their two children, so what could she do?

She could shut up and try to be a good parson's wife, a mother and a housekeeper, living her life on two levels. Alan was possibly doing good rather than harm by preaching about his shadowy inefficient god; and by his kind, anxious, gentle relations with people he was doing much good and no harm at all. He did know his people. He had been able to answer at once about Gault and Howlett.

But he had not squared up his god with container-lorries and little kids on bikes.

He was living in a picturesque tradition, and not a very old one: as the stars saw Time, it was only yesterday that the C. of E. usurped the premises and the culture of the R.C. Church in Britain, and only the day before yesterday there had been Druids. Now there was a new god, money. And just as it was useless to supplicate a god who wasn't there, it was equally useless to supplicate a blind, deaf and stupid appetite. The romantic legendary god had faded out and the new one was just as much the product of Man's desires – how else could a god be made? – but the nature of the men who made him had deteriorated. Helen thought her world was in a profound trough of disillusion. But with so much cooking and housework to do, and parochial fêtes, jumble sales, Mothers' Union meetings and so forth and so on demanding her attention, and not only that, her presence in person, she had little time to worry about religion. The parochial nonsense was not religion, it was dedicated to the great god Money, and was rather humiliating when one considered the vast riches of the Church Commissioners. Anyone could discover by inquiry in the right quarter that the Commissioners, with their Stock Exchange portfolio plus enormous possessions in land, houses and city premises, were among the biggest millionaires in Britain.

Helen felt ashamed when her duty as a parson's wife called upon her to beg for money or goods to augment such riches. But she never told her thoughts: what good could she have done, against Alan's unquestioning faith that all was for the best in the best of all possible worlds; and against the embattled power of a State Church?

She was committed to serve her husband and children as best she could; this included keeping her opinions to herself. And teaching the children to say their prayers. To whom were these addressed? It could not matter. Praying was in itself a harmless palliative. Casting all your cares upon Him for He careth for you. Oh, that it were so!

Oh that some Power, a true, active, powerful Power, would look down on little kids bicycling to school, at that complicated main-road crossing!

5
Transients

A leading authority on squatting in East Anglia had advised Bob Hammer, 'Try the Radmere area. There's a lot of building of small houses on the north side of the river, and that often means empty big houses, nobody wanting them now.'

Bob Hammer set off in his rattly old pick-up, his wife and child beside him and nothing much in the body of the pick-up except an even more rattly old pram, two suitcases, a large enamel basin, a frying pan and a sleeping-bag. The Hammers were at a low ebb. Their London squat had proved not only too expensive in food and drink but also uncongenial. The other people in the house had kept themselves and their money and goods *to* themselves – no sense of community. Bob Hammer wanted to live in a Commune based firmly on love and work, but that one in North London had had neither love nor work. Bob knew he had nothing but what he could scrounge from the Welfare State to contribute to the cost of buying things for communal living, but he was a strong and practical chap, he could saw logs, he could dig . . . well, he could saw logs if there was wood to saw and a saw to do it with, and he could dig like anything but he didn't know what or how to plant in the ground he had dug. He had always longed to be a country lad – his mother had been the child of many country generations – but he had had no opportunity.

Now, with the tentative backing of two other families, two single chaps and the squat-expert, he was hoping to found a true Commune, based on love and work. Since he was the only owner of motor transport, salvaged from a scrapyard at the cost of a week's Public Assistance, it had fallen to him to go exploring. The assignment appealed to him, the country-lover. It appealed far less to his very young wife Kerry. Luckily the baby liked motoring. After the final row with the bourgeoisie in the North London squat, he could not have left Kerry and the baby behind. Kerry just didn't have what it took to defend the Commune ideal. Well, how could she? She had only just achieved elementary reading and writing at sixteen when he married her because she was so sweet and pretty.

This was how the Gants Hall Commune came into being. The expert had been right. A gaunt red fancy-built late-Victorian mansion stood vacant, with not even an agent's FOR SALE or TO LET notice on it, on a by-road somewhere north of a quite large village-extension of little neat houses, scores of them, for sale at nine to twelve thousand pounds each. The Hammers had no pounds, nor did Bob want that bourgeois kind of life. It never occurred to him to ask what Kerry wanted.

All the lower windows of the mansion were broken. There was no problem about getting in. If one did not fancy a jagged ground-floor window, the paintless front-door panels were rotted by rain.

There was almost nothing in the house which could be called furniture. The kitchen had a large black cooking range and sufficient built-in cupboards, and up in the palatial bathroom there was a huge bath and a loo on a sort of pedestal.

Outside, there was a biggish garden front and back, fenced in by straggling uncut thorns and totally overgrown by brambles and nettles. Bob flexed his muscles.

It was necessary to find out a few basic facts. Village pubs were the places for finding out, but this gaunt red house was away from any village, and where was the pub? By sheer luck Bob found an ancient leaning over the gate of a cottage garden.

'That owd pleace? Empty these ten year and nobody know who own that. Reckon do the owner could be found, Council 'ud buy that, rock-bottom proice, for demolition and a lot more o' them-there tiddly lil expensive housen. But you can't demolish what ain't yourn, exceptin' there's a war on.'

Bob sorted out this information. And without further ado, a house empty for ten years and neither for sale nor to let appearing safe enough, entered in and took over two ground-floor rooms – use of kit. and bath to be understood by all other potential occupants. He then had to spend some pence telephoning to his supporters. That was how the Gants Hall Commune started.

Three weeks saw the house full. Some had brought furniture in hired vans. On the left of the front door a family called Porter, Pa, Ma, two kids and another on the way, took two rooms and filled them with beds, chairs, a table, a sofa, all the middle-class stuff. Bob and Kerry had already staked their claim to the corresponding two rooms on the right of the front door but they had almost nothing to call furniture.

Never mind, this was to be a Commune. If you wanted to sit on a sofa, no one cared who owned the sofa, it was everyone's, just as Bob's pick-up truck and his willingness to work was everyone's. Not everybody understood Communism but Bob did. He would put in all he'd got, which wasn't much, and if others put in more it was simply because they *had* more. All put in their all, for all.

And all worked for all. In theory, for love of all.

The two single males, Angus in his forties, Jem younger, walked around holding hands or arms-round-necks. Very young Kerry Hammer expressed disgust. Bob told her patiently, 'A lot of people, and not men only, are born like that. It just happens and they have to adjust to it: and lucky if they find the right person to live with. I don't know who started calling them "gay" – it's not often the right word. But those two look very contented, and they've been together a long time. Among the few lucky ones, I'd say.'

'It gives me the creeps.'

'It's not your business, Kerry. Have the creeps if you like. Nobody cares.'

Bob had never before spoken to her so sharply and coldly. They had had quick short shouting-matches, decibels equal and reconciliation immediate – mostly about the baby – but this steel flick-knife had shot out of nowhere. Kerry simply did not know how she had offended so gravely.

She was too young, just seventeen. Bob had been around six years longer than Kerry: he had also been better at absorbing both education and the things which his own observation told him.

The two single men chose a couple of large attics for bedroom and sitter and immediately began cleaning up and making habitable their eyrie. They had chosen better than some (they were not handicapped, of course, by babies) in that their windows, so high up, were not broken. A hired truck had brought a spring mattress and bedding, a couple of floor-rugs, an oil cooker and other bare necessities: in fact they could have lived upstairs and disappeared from mortal ken, which Bob had supposed to be their objective. But not so. Angus was a carpenter and Jem was a super cook.

'They pull their weight all right,' said the elderly Strangs, who had reason to know, having had their windows backed over with transparent polythene at no cost to themselves. 'It's perhaps a pity that some of the others don't. Not that we can talk; we're old and rather helpless except that we can contribute our pensions.' It seemed that Bob Hammer, who had discovered the house, was to be regarded – no, not as boss, Communes didn't have bosses, but as consultant.

No one expected the pregnant women and the mothers of small children to do much beyond looking after their men and their brats. But they could have done some washing!

Washing? With no hot water except what you boiled on the kitchen range or cooked up on that terrifying geyser over the bath?

No one had any baths. The obsession with bodily cleanliness was, after all, bourgeois. Aristocrats and workers stank; only the blighted Middle Class was obsessed with the body. But small untrained babies (pot-training being bourgeois) demanded clean or semi-clean nappies. And the first big row occurred when the bath was found to be full of unwashed Porter nappies when Kerry Hammer wanted to wash those of her own baby.

Kerry stormed downstairs and bashed on the Porter door. A skim-milk-faced Jane Porter peered out.

'Hell,' yelled Kerry, 'when are you going to get your kids' filthy nappies out of the bath? Where am I to wash *my* kid's nappies? Have you paid rent for the bathroom or something?'

'Oh, Mrs Hammer, I feel so sick when I have to wash nappies.'

'No one ever tell you how to stop getting pregnant? Use your loaf or make your stupid man who can't even help in the garden use his. You don't *have* to be pregnant every nine months, you silly cow.' Kerry was informed on the basics, though not yet experienced in social life.

But Mrs Porter did have to be pregnant every nine, ten or eleven months. The Porters were Catholics. Not the best people to try to live in a Commune, they demanded too much, for their too many children.

The nappy business was the real break-up of the Commune. Not the pair of male homos, who had endeared themselves by practical work and by readiness to baby-sit (babies loved them). Even Kerry Hammer had come round.

No, the worm at the root of the Commune was laziness. Some, like Bob, Angus and Jem, were ready and willing to work at anything they could do. If progress at making and mending, digging and planting was not rapid, it was because materials had to be bought and money had to be spent mainly on food. But those perpetually pregnant Porters, the woman a breeding sow and the man an unpublished writer, never contributed anything – money, work or even love – to the public store. Jem, Kerry and old Mrs Grant, the cooks, cooked for the Porters, the same meals as the rest had, take it or leave it. Anyone who wanted anything special had to cook it (and pay for it) himself. Mrs Porter felt too ill to cook, and Mr had no ideas about paying for anything, so the Porters either ate or did not eat from the communal pot, for which the others had paid. It was known that the Porters extracted what they could from the Welfare State, as the rest did. But it took a surgical operation with a cork-screw, Angus the Scot said, tipping an imaginary glass, to get Porter's share of the paraffin bill out of him: or the petrol bill for Bob's pick-up which was the only contact with shop, post office, doctor's surgery, the outside world in general. The only people in the house who would walk more than a hundred yards were Angus and Jem.

The Porters contributed the money which was forced out of them – almost with menaces. But money was not the only thing needed. What about love and work?

But how did one set about expelling the Porters? Bob asked himself. None of the families or near-families paid any rent, so no one could be evicted for non-payment of rent. Except by sheer force, no one could be evicted for anything. None of the Commune had any legal rights – the whole thing was illegal.

Bob Hammer was generally held to be the originator of the Commune, though his contributions had been limited to his extortions from the Welfare State and his nearly useless efforts with saw and spade. (Wishing to do real work was not the same as doing it.) Bob had begun to hate the Porters – in a Commune where Love was the word – because they were lazy and dirty. He knew that laziness and dirt were no disqualifications for belonging to the human race; some people were lazy and dirty: one had to love them regardless. But Bob couldn't. Poor young Kerry had to boil kettles to wash nappies in her only basin, because the bathroom was always filthy and stinking with Porters. Bob had stopped rebuking Kerry for bourgeois ideas: he'd had to, because his baby had no ideas at all, it just kept wetting and dirtying its nappies, or when it ran out of nappies, its pants and the floor, and Kerry just had to do something about it. Bob, his head in Communist clouds, had never known how wet and dirty babies were.

You just could not have lazy filthy Porters in a Commune. They would have to take their chairs, their sofa, their table, their bed (more than any of the others had) somewhere else. Kerry was not the only one who complained about the disgusting bathroom, but she was the most aggrieved because she too had a baby. Bob reasoned it out. Her fuss was not only because of bourgeois notions of cleanliness, it was about the baby's health and happiness, and one couldn't accuse a baby of having false ideas of propriety. The struggle in Bob's mind between dogma and common sense was almost visible.

Angus the senior homo helped him out. 'Those people must go or else we do; and we contribute more and make no bloody mess.'

'Angus, it's against my principles to deny the rights of any people to be as they are.'

'Look, laddie, they are not the dregs of Glasgow slums who've had no chance to learn better: one could want to help those. The Porters don't need help, they need guts, and they haven't any. They're middle-class parasites. Living on *us*. And I know you don't have much to spare, old man.'

Bob was silent.

'OK,' said Angus, 'Jem and I move out, Spencer and his doll will move out too, and the old Grants are fed to the back teeth I can tell you. So's your poor little wife. Have you thought of her?'

Bob was silent.

'We'll all go, leaving you with Kerry and the kid, and the filthy Porters with their two and another any minute. The Porters will go on spreading their muck all over the place (did you know the loo was blocked with sanitary towels?) and you and Kerry will have to cope, cooking for the Porters as well as yourselves: we all cook for the Porters, don't we? A Commune is a holiday for the Porters. Look, Bob, if you can't or daren't heave them out, leave them on their own. Find some other place. You'll always be welcome with Jem and me.'

'And you two with us,' said Bob, though unable to disguise his sadness at the break-up of his first Commune. One ought not to have to vet people: all had the right to be alive and to be cared for . . . even lazy dirty Porters. But.

Those who left that melancholy house, its broken windows merely tacked-over with cardboard or polythene, its unproductive nettly garden and its long distance from any shop were not sorry to go. There had been other drawbacks besides the Porters.

Finding themselves deserted and therefore helpless, the Porters went too, with their furniture and no nappies – they would buy some throw-away ones en route. The Commune vanished, having done nothing in the catchment area except mulct the taxpayers of everything available from the Welfare State and the National Health Service.

On the south edge of the area lived Herbert Macrow, known to the natives as Harbutt, as in Plasticine, and Macro as in macrobiotics. Harbutt was a chap with an eye for opportunity but not often enough money to make the most of opportunity. Harbutt had had his eye on an empty and decaying double-cottage with half an acre of land at the edge of one of the several commons in Colham village. He went more than once to the owner, young Mr Brandling, forcing tears to his eyes while he told the tale of his lonely mother-in-law who would be so happy to live within reach of her daughter. The Macrows lived three miles away in the next village.

Jonathan Brandling said, 'Can't the old girl live with you? She'll be some way off, at that cottage.'

'God forbid,' said Harbutt; 'you surely know about mothers-in-law, Mr Brandling.'

Jonathan did not know but had the theoretic fear. To him it was a pity that men had to have women around at all. A wife, however, had many uses. It was certainly difficult to see much good in a ma-in-law. He felt sympathy with Harbutt. Also, the decaying cottage was no use to the Brandling farms, since the drastic reduction in manpower in favour of machine-power brought about by Jonathan himself after he became the effective manager of the farms.

Eventually, because of Harbutt's importunity he gave in and sold the large cottage and its half-acre at no fancy price to the man of opportunity.

Who immediately put a new thatched roof on it, colour-washed the outside, and put it up for sale at nineteen thousand pounds. He had never had a mother-in-law. She had departed this life in faith and fear before ever he married.

No one was idiot enough to buy the cottage, even with its half-acre, at that price, with the inside unmodernized and quite horrible. Harbutt had to wait for more money, before improving the inside. But suddenly he received an offer to rent the place, from a group of self-styled musicians, the bearded young men wearing jeans and fancy coats edged with straggly goat-hair, the girls wearing long full dresses to disguise pregnancy. There was money there: huge musical instruments cost a bit. Besides, one of the young men dished out a month's rent in advance. Harbutt had not liked to charge more than five pounds a week for a place full of dry-rot and wood-worm and empty of furniture except for the kitchen range. Furthermore he was afraid of losing five pounds a week by asking for ten.

He was sorry when he discovered that the steady population of the cottage was eleven, with more at weekends. He ought to have demanded at least ten pounds. His wife kept on at him about it.

The young startlingly-dressed people, the men so hairy that one set of small pink features hiding in a bush was indistinguishable from another, the girls with green eye-sockets and white lips, were cooked for by a jolly middle-aged lady in a torn nightdress. They had a van to take them to Radmere for shopping and for two of their number to collect Public Assistance: also to take the Group to provide noise at dances not too far away. The lot of them caused no trouble to anyone except when the wind set in the wrong way at nights. Apparently they could only practise their noise around midnight: and it was a very loud noise which disturbed people, who needed their sleep because they worked as early as daylight permitted, within a mile either side of the cottage, depending on the set of the wind. Country people sleep through country noises except the wrong 'uns, the bellowing of cattle escaped from their familiar fields, the soprano yap of a fox after someone's hand-reared pheasant poults. But they do not sleep through strange crashing, banging, wailing, shouting 'music'.

Nobody made any formal complaint. The young people were harmless and very civil when given the sele of the day. They seemed to be as clean as they could be in their primitive circumstances – washing always flew on the line outside the cottage.

A baby arrived soon after the Group moved in, and nappies flew on the line. The countryman is tolerant of anything which seems to him natural and unavoidable, such as babies and nappies and even barking dogs and escaping cattle; he only arises in his might against manifest injustice. The crowd at the cottage, though they did not mix because they did not want to, were indulgently accepted because they did no harm.

But they flitted, all of them, as soon as the new baby (whose? The village did not know) was old enough for a journey. The word was, they had found a larger and better place in Essex, handier for shopping and offering larger towns and villages where the Group could play so-called music for so-called dancing. Off they all went in two furniture-vans, no expense spared, leaving Harbutt minus five pounds a week and much disturbed by something else.

'Did you know,' asked one of the local reporter-boys, the departure of the Group being news of a sort, 'that the chap who did all the paying, the one with the percussion outfit, was a relation of the Royals?'

'*What?*'

'That's the word going round. After all, there had to be some money, only two of them were on the State. They paid your rent and they paid their food-bills and petrol et cetera in the town, and they've gone to a much bigger place in Essex – I'll try to find out where, and what the rent is, just as a matter of interest. They *are* interesting. But what are you going to do with that double-cottage?'

'Give me time. I'll make it right inside and sell it for twenty thousand. The piece of land with it is good for building, after all.'

'You wouldn't like to tell me what you paid young Mr Brandling for it?'

'I bloody well wouldn't. It's nobody's business but mine,' said Harbutt.

'I'm not so sure,' said Colin the apprentice reporter. 'Money is news, these days.'

'Are you suggesting there's something wrong?'

'Good God, no, all sorts of fiddles are perfectly legal,' said Colin, and left Harbutt nervously wondering. But he felt reassured, though not at all happy, by a rough computation of what it would cost him to put water, bathroom, lavatory and all that into the cottage, and re-lay the dry-rotted floors and probably the wood-wormed rafters. If and when he did all that, he would not see a dishonest profit out of it; he'd be lucky to see the kind of profit which had come to be regarded as normal, say a couple of thousand pounds.

Meanwhile the cottage sat there empty and silent and

rotting, the gay-plumaged songbirds flown. Songbirds? Parakeets, more like. But they had kept the house warmed by the kitchen range. Standing empty did a house no good.

The Group had mulcted the catchment area of no more than two Social Security payments over several months and a National Health attendance at the birth of the baby. The lady in the nightdress had in fact saved the State something by her practical service at the birth of her grandson, reputed to be the newest arrival in the now very widespread Royal Family. Hundredth in succession to the throne?

Communes come in all sizes and all grades. They come and they go. Real country life in a place of small population and less amenity, such as the catchment area, is usually more than they can stand.

6
Male Chauvinist Pigdom

Janey Peters, who knew the Gaults slightly through the
Area Conservative Association, read about the Court case
and wished she could discuss it with her brother, who had
once known the Brigadier pretty well, having been treasurer
while the Brig was chairman; but who had now no memories
save capriciously selected ones of his early childhood,
mostly before Janey was born. So each spoke in riddles to
the other, and Janey had to keep her lively interest stored
up in her bosom until she happened to meet Harriet Brandling in the Radmere supermarket. The queues at the check-
out points were immensely long. Men as well as women had
push-carts full of everything, for it was market day and from
the wide area served by Radmere (which stood at a central
point roughly twenty miles from any larger town) villagers
had come in by bus and car. The town was crammed. The
market place, with the great church at the top, was massed

with stalls under awnings, selling fruit and vegetables, clothes, cakes, garden plants, household linens and holy books. The stalls were no cheaper than the shops, but they seemed cheaper because they were in the open air. Old women like Janey and Harriet (and apparently lots of others of both sexes, not all of them old) found it less tiring, though not much, to shop under one roof. The tiring part came at the check-out.

Janey and Harriet had a long time to wait while trolleys stacked high and wire-baskets heaped up were shunted down the line, checked and paid for.

Harriet had only an extensive variety of cat-food. Her weekends were governed by the idiosyncrasies of cats. Stinker ate anything, Sandy was pernickety, Fluffo erratic, and tiny baby Sausage, bereft of its mother by some passing motor vehicle, ate very little. Shopping for the cats was far more difficult than shopping for Harold. Janey had been buying cotton-wool bread and canned meat and fruit, because Jimmy, like Stinker, had to be filled up with something, no matter what.

'Oh, Mrs Brandling, how nice to see you. *Why* do we do this? Things are only the odd penny dearer at our village shops.'

'Ah, but your village isn't my village,' said Harriet. 'It's nice to come to town now and then and stop twenty times in the street to give the sele of the day to people one would never see otherwise. I'd never see *you*, except once a year at some party, but for Radmere Market Day.'

'That's true. Look, while we have the time, what do you think of our friends at Willington Green?' asked Janey.

'The Gaults? No friends of mine, I'm the wrong Party,' said Harriet. 'But I've always been sorry for little sat-upon Missis, and I'm sorrier than ever now. There ought to be a society for the protection of sat-upon wives.'

'There's one being formed for battered wives.'

'You don't have to be battered. The bruises don't show: they're deep in the soul: but you're a destroyed creature just the same.'

'Do you know she's sat-upon? She's very silent, of course, but it could be because she's got nothing to say,' suggested Janey.

'I know a few things. She loves dogs and has never been allowed to have one; there's a bush-telegraph between us doggy people. And another thing: I've seen her blasted husband make her look silly at an innocent cocktail party, and I've heard him contradict her *but flatly* more than once in public – "See what fools women are" sort of thing. She's a nothing to him and he sees to it that she's a nothing to anyone else. She's his chattel like the "property" he was on about in Court. His own. He bought it. He bought her, in the days when helpless girls of gentle birth went out to India with the fishing fleet and caught husbands, no matter how ghastly, to keep them, no matter how miserably, from the shameful necessity of having to earn money by work.'

'Is that really so, Harriet?'

'Two friends of mine, playing about at Oxford without much talent or purpose, took ship. Both caught disastrous men. So did poor little Mrs Gault. How long, Lord, how long, before women realize that they have a *choice?*'

'I chose mine,' said Janey, 'but he was killed in the First World War. We'd only had a few days together, both of us in our teens. I didn't even manage a baby.'

'Bloody bad luck,' said Harriet. 'I chose mine too, and he's still going strong, though not quite the man I chose. Bad luck for me as well, actually. But he was never the one to make me afraid or dumb like poor Irene Gault.'

'I can't imagine you,' said Janey, 'ever afraid or dumb.'

'True enough, I'm not easily cowed. I've always paid

my way, that's why. But the fishing-fleet women, they had no reserves of strength. They went husband-hunting because they were so weak.'

'Well, they don't go to India any more,' said Janey. 'Where can they go now, the brainless victims of brainless parents, the upper-middle-class gals?'

'Maybe quite a lot of them have discovered they can earn enough to live on as secretaries or models or what-not without selling themselves to husbands to escape the unspoken anxieties of parents; and not always unspoken. Oh, look, the queue's beginning to move.'

This was the intermittent friendship between Harriet and Janey, that when they met, though rarely and briefly, they could at once establish common ground and talk sense, which was better than wasting precious minutes on the weather, their rheumatics, and the price of food. And since they never reached the end of a subject and packed it away, they gave each other food for further thought. Two old but still lively women in a stagnant backwater. Two old frogs croaking away in a dirty little pond, was Janey's version. But Harriet did not miscall the pond; the rich life in its mud fed her mind.

On the evenings of market days, most of the ladies in the Radmere catchment area who wanted an 'out' from cooking, washing and housework went to flower-arranging classes. There were books and books in the Public Library about this activity, so they felt intellectual, though actually they were, in varying degrees, frustrated artists, having had no opportunity to develop any artistic gift until such time as their children could be left to the tender mercies of Daddy – or were grown up and gone. Flower-arranging was a way of creating something which was not a meal or a baby. Of those they had had enough, any more of those would call for sheer endurance. But an arrangement of flowers was both more beautiful and far less trouble or expense. And was a mental and moral tonic.

One of the newer members of the Radmere Flower Club was Clara Howlett. Her husband made no bones about chauffeuring her into town most weeks for the evening meetings, because flower decoration fitted in with his ambitions for his garden and was also a breach in the walls of the Middle Class. Furthermore he himself enjoyed a drink in a pub which was not full of the local yokels of Willington Green, so he could fill in the time while she was at her meetings by talking of impersonal matters to men who were not his neighbours. Essentially a public man, he preferred, even as his enemy the Brigadier did though with more knowledge of this present world, his private life to be his own. Thus far, the people with whom he had had conversations of all degrees of seriousness in the numerous Radmere pubs did not even know his name or place of abode.

After the Court case this was a distinct advantage. Had they known him they'd have circled warily round him and poked leading questions at him, and would have been quite unwilling to discuss inflation, Stonehouse, Prentice or the Common Market.

But Clara's name and address were noted down in the minutes of the Flower Club. Her appearance at the meeting quite soon after the Court case caused a dead silence, because no one knew what to say to a wife whose husband had been bound over in a large sum to keep the peace because of threats of arson. (There was no worry about the other wife, whose husband had shot-off his twelve bore in a highly irresponsible manner, because Irene Gault had never been allowed to belong to anything in which her husband was not also interested.)

And some of the ladies were worried about Clara's dear dog. Could they ask if it was still alive?

There were those whose true thoughts were: 'How ghastly to have a husband with such a temper – and that goes for the old military person as well!' There were those who thought chiefly about the poor innocent dog. There was not one who knew how to broach the subject or how to avoid it. Naturally they all wanted first-hand information which would make them centres of interest for at least a fortnight.

Clara Howlett, though she had never been allowed to learn to drive a car, was a woman of sense and humour. She had expected the sudden silence at her well-timed entry, neither early nor late, into the school hall; she knew just what the other ladies had been thinking and saying. So she found her place at one of the tables on which the competition, 'Early Summer' was to be set out, laid down the handsome bunch of her husband's flowers which she had been carrying, and smiled round upon her silent co-workers.

'I suppose you've all read about our fracas at Willington Green?' she asked pleasantly. And another woman with a good social sense immediately replied,

'Oh, yes, your dog's not badly hurt, is he? I do hope not.' That was the easy way in.

'No, he's OK. That's a nice kind vet we have. What *isn't* OK is the war between those two awful men. They're bound over but they don't *feel* peaceful. I just wonder what'll happen next, and I can't prevent mine, nor can poor Mrs Gault prevent hers. They're both male chauvinist pigs.'

By now most of the ladies had gathered round. So there was no awkwardness after all, in chatting to the wife of the potential incendiarist, even on that very subject. Most of the husbands were, or had been when alive, male chauvinist pigs, and the two or three spinsters were quite ready to take the same line since it provided a good excuse for spinsterhood. Clara had acquired her social sense from being a great joiner of all kinds of clubs and societies within bus-distance of her city suburb. She had learnt how best to break the silence of the polite, nervous Radmere ladies by being easy, forthright and truthful. She was not troubled by any feeling that she ought to stick up for her spouse come Hell or high water: in her simple view, men had their daft side (I mean, she would say, look at Rugger and boxing and, come to that, war) and why should a sensible person support madness?

Poor little Mrs Gault did not belong to the Flower Club. It was the sort of thing to which the Brigadier said Pshaw or its equivalent. Damn' silly women fiddling with damn' useless flowers. The Gault garden produced only food. The Brigadier belonged to the Horticultural Society and regularly won prizes at the quarterly show, but seldom felt the need to go to weekly meetings to learn about fertilizers and aphids, and if he had, the meetings would not have coincided with those of the Flower Club. A special journey in his big old car for the benefit of Irene and no benefit to himself was out of the question. She could go with him to the weekly Bridge Club at Barringer or his weekly chess with the parson at Pye, or of course the Conservative Club at Radmere; but considering the price of petrol, that was enough. Who would waste the precious juice on damn' silly women fiddling with damn' useless flowers?

Irene hated bridge: the post-mortems were so humiliating. She was not at all sure that she was a Conservative, and was too stupid ever to have learnt to play chess, for which she was thankful. But she was quite good with the wild flowers which were the only ones she had. She arranged them in the house with love and joy, though the only person who noticed them was the woman from across the Green who came on Mondays to do the washing, and who said she couldn't understand why Irene cluttered the place up with them weeds.

But one had to love something, and she was not allowed dog or cat so she loved wild flowers and had become very well informed about them, not that anybody cared. The village was far enough away from Radmere to warrant a Mobile Library, to which Irene submitted requests (you don't give orders to the Library Service, although you pay rates) for books on botany, particularly on wild flowers and native trees and shrubs. The Brig never knew that there was one subject on which his poor silly wife was an authority while he was an ignoramus.

Irene Gault, of course, was not at that Flower Club meeting, but if she had been, Clara Howlett would have been just as frank, without injuring Irene in any way. The two of them were allies against male chauvinist pigdom.

Their acquisition of their respective males had run on very different courses. Irene had had a so-called and highly expensive education at a school full of Honourables, and had then Come Out, unqualified for any other profession than Coming Out, the upper-class version of street-walking. A Major, handsome, dominating, uniformed, had saved her parents the trouble and expense of sending her out with the fishing fleet. *Reader, she married him*, and regretted it ever after.

He married her because she was a lady, right accent, right 'pretty' looks, and stupidity as putty-like as any Army officer could ask of any lady.

The education of a lady, at most of the expensive private schools open to her parents' money fifty years ago, was quite different from that of a woman. Only young ladies were accepted, young women went to State schools. A girl at an expensive private school had to be very intelligent and very strong, to resist the young-lady nonsense and emerge as a young woman with brains. Irene had not been strong enough. She had emerged with no qualifications except ladyhood. By 1975–6 she was a dumb old greying blonde who had no idea how to cash in on her special botanical knowledge and had never been allowed by her male chauvinistic pig to have a dog. She had been born and educated to be kept and dictated to by a male chauvinist pig.

Her friend Clara Howlett had reached Grammar School but had only obtained one A-level, in Domestic Science, which enabled her to shop intelligently and cook digestibly for her own male chauvinist pig. Clara was rather better off, for free, than Irene, after heavy expenditure, had been. Irene was a nothing, merely a lady, replaceable. There were still some overspills from the era of ladies, even in 1975. But there was no overspill of qualified cooks and house-keepers.

The Grammar School domestic science courses had not kept up with the demand; perhaps they never would. The men lucky enough to marry girls who could cook and shop, if these girls also had brains and opinions of their own had to bear with them. The Brigadier had not had to endure a clever wife; he had had to pay, instead, for a washing-woman, a scrubbing-woman and a general sweeping-and-cleaning-woman from the village. He called them 'these people' as though they were ants and was very angry if he caught Irene drinking tea with any one of them.

One of the flower ladies working alongside Clara Howlett was a pretty young-married. The number of young was small, because as soon as they married and had houses, or even if they did not marry and have houses, they had children. It would be several years before, married or single, they would be free to attend meetings from seven to nine p.m., to learn how to beautify houses by flower-arrangements.

Alma Beech was a girl who traded on her looks. The danger was that she would try to go on doing it after she had lost them. She sidled up to Clara Howlett with a dancing step and said, 'Will your husband really set the General's house on fire?'

'I wouldn't be surprised, if the old boy shoots at him or at my dog again,' said Clara, 'and I wouldn't blame him.'

'But it's a gorgeous old thatched house and it's the General's *property*.'

'My husband may not be a gorgeous old thatched house, but his life is *his* property and my dog is *my* property,' said Clara. 'Do you think a sixteenth-century house is worth more than a man's life, or even a dog's? I don't. It's up to the old boy anyway, he starts the trouble, he's the one with the gun.'

Alma blinked her huge blue eyes, with their unnatural green lids and artificial eyelashes, at Clara. She always painted her face all over and did her eyes, even for the old pussies at the Flower Arrangement, because she would have felt naked without these aids, just as she would have felt a dwarf without seven-inch heels and two-and-a-half-inch soles on her shoes, just about the highest you could buy. Clara thought it was difficult to see what the silly kid really looked like, and perhaps that was why she disguised herself. She could be a little runt with no eyelashes and the ghastly green might be meant to put protuberant eyes back into their sockets – but it did not succeed. The girl looked like a clown not very good at walking on stilts. Was that what she wanted?

Well, thought Clara, thinking of her distant marriage to her male chauvinist pig, I've been silly in some ways but this lot is silly all along the line.

'Did he really shoot at your husband, Mrs Howlett?'

'Really truly, after peppering my poor dog, but fortunately he couldn't hit a haystack at twenty yards,' said Clara, addressing herself to her flower-picture and hoping she had trimmed up young Mrs Beech's picture of high-ranking Army officers. What did a kid of nineteen know about anything?

Young Alma knew enough to snatch the second prize

from Mrs Howlett, but Clara did not grudge this. To her, playing with flowers was a pleasing recreation. Some people happily played ball-games without stunning success; Clara could play flower-games. They were sociable, and occasionally produced a small masterpiece, just as garden-party tennis, in the days when that other wife, Irene Gault, was young, occasionally produced the totally satisfying shot. Clara was ten years younger than her friend Irene, but they had the same ideas about enjoyment, however different their backgrounds and schooling.

Clara said to the secretary, 'Has Mrs Gault ever been asked to be a member? She's clever with flowers.'

'Oh, I think she was asked, when we started, before I was secretary. Let's look.' The secretary riffled the pages of the minute-book. 'Oh, yes, here's the very first committee-meeting. Mrs Gault was among those to be asked.' A page or two later came the answer. Mrs Gault had written to say she could not join the club because she had no means of attending the meetings.

'Male chauvinist pig,' said Clara Howlett. The secretary did not quite catch the allusion.

7

Old Men in the Chimney-Corner

It was not exactly a chimney-corner, it was a very old-established eating-house, almost a coffee-house, in Radmere, where throughout living memory men – mostly men – had popped in on market day from the Corn Hall across the way for elevenses, and later for great satisfying plates of cold beef, any time between noon and one o'clock, to keep them alive until they got home for high tea around six (to be followed by cocoa, sandwiches and pastries at any hour up to ten o'clock.)

The rise into the Middle Class and the consequent change in eating fashions had gradually altered the customers at this very good-value but non-alcoholic source of food and conversation. Some farmers, by the nineteen-seventies, even had Late Dinner, and most of them could afford something more expensive than tea or coffee to drink with their meals; or even if they could not afford it, they thought they ought to, to make a good impression upon those agents for machinery, seeds or what-not whom they entertained to 'lunch' at licensed houses. (Occasionally it was the agents who entertained the farmers. Either way, it meant a decline in the prosperity of the very old Coffee House.)

One of those old customers who held on until death was Harold Brandling – while Harriet waited in the car and hoped she would have time to cook the mid-day dinner which Harold had had since he had teeth wherewith to eat it. Harold had a cup of tea, and to him came sometimes, not always, those cronies who were still alive. Most of his companions of cricket matches and shooting parties were now dead. Too many times, his ritual cuppa yielded nothing in reminiscence, gossip or even remarks upon the weather. Often there was simply nobody else present, often some man or couple at the far end of the room, who had no idea who the white-haired old josser in the shabby clothes might be. Harold's world was full of 'new' people in all walks of life. People who had never known him, as employer, as customer, as slow-bowler or as friend.

To him entered a seafaring man, of indeterminate age – sun and sea-wind make deep engravings on faces – but a Senior Citizen without a doubt, wearing a knitted cap with a bobble on top and a hefty but perfectly clean white fisherman-type jersey. Also, of course, a pair of trousers. This man, among very few, felt some responsibility for entertaining that poor old relic, Harold Brandling.

The weather dealt with, he said, 'Did I ever tell you about my trip to Yarmouth when I was eight?'

'No, what about it?' Harold gladly listened to anything, and did not actually forget what he heard; rather, it stowed itself away among the accumulation of junk in the back of his mind, and was hard to unearth when wanted.

'I remembered it in bed last night and it made me laugh.

We do remember our childhood when we get old, don't you find?' said the sailorman, who was not in fact a sailorman but one of a different trade who merely loved the sea and had spent his spare time on it, as so many East Anglians do.

'Well, it was like this. I was on my own, a very little boy in a train-load of grown-ups not responsible for me. I knew where I was meant to go – I had an auntie in Yarmouth. But it was a long and twisty way from the Beach Station to my auntie's, so I did a clever thing, I filled my pockets with rice from my mother's kitchen cupboard, and when I left Beach Station I kept asking the way, as I'd been told to do, and dribbled a trail of rice after me to show me the way back. Smart, wasn't it? But not smart enough. After a long way, I asked a kind lady if I was on the right bearing, and she said to go back to the last turning. So I swung round, and blow me down if a whole fleet of ruddy pigeons wasn't on my heels, gobbling up every grain.'

Old man Brandling laughed his near-silent laugh. The story was a success, but it was not quite done. 'And d'you know what the old gal said? "Such a nice kind boy to feed the dear birds!" I didn't tell her how wrong she was. My auntie, poor thing, had to lug me all the way back to Beach Station to get the train home.'

Harold Brandling's in-fallen lipless mouth was no asset in repose but his face was greatly altered by a smile. The seafaring man felt he had done a bit of good. Some people never did any. It might be counted unto him at the last day: he'd need it.

Harold paid for his cup of tea and shoogled down the street towards Harriet's usual parking place. If she had not found a spot, where would the car be? It was a daily worry, but the cup of tea was the main thing, because Harold had had it for years and years. If Harriet was not where she ought to be, how could he go from car to car in the dozen possible parking places, large and small, in the town? His legs would not take him.

She was there, waiting, sitting staring before her in the driving seat of her car. Good. (He did not know how good it was for Harriet too, to glimpse him in her driving-mirror, heading the right way. Janey Peters had told her about losing Jimmy more than once.)

While Harold still remembered it, he would tell Harriet the funny story. He did so and they chuckled over it. Harriet just stopped herself from saying 'I'm glad you found someone to talk to': it would have underlined the fact that nine days out of ten he found nobody. She said, 'He's an amusing fellow,' keeping back for a similar reason the word she could have added, 'kind-hearted'. She kept trying not to accentuate the isolation of Harold's extreme old age; he would not like to think that other people (even his wife) observed his plight. He had his pride.

Harriet knew, though if Harold had been warned he had forgotten, that the time was coming when cataracts and deafness would wipe out all pride; when a man would be grateful for a plate of invisible food to push haphazard into his mouth. Whether it was palatable or not, it would be food.

And Harriet knew, though Harold certainly did not, that when that time came, she, though younger, might have left him. He'd be on his own in the silent dark but still alive. Tough as an old boot and just about as intelligent. Whereas Harriet was in less good physical condition and had a jumpy heart. She did not worry about it on her own account – she was not over-attached to life. She had done her work, her children were settled and capable. While she sat and waited in her car, it was about poor old Harold that she worried, who could not relinquish the half-life he led, the mind gone, the knowledge of affairs gone, the muscles for the cricket and shooting gone, everything gone but food, television

and sleep. She often thought her heart-condition, whatever
it was (silly expression: everything at all times had a condition
of some sort) might let her off duty before Harold became a
ninety-year-old baby.

There was nothing to be said in praise of extreme old age.
It was not clever, admirable or economic to go on living
after one had done one's stuff. Harriet had her departure all
fixed except the date: a letter to the Coroner so that her
remains need not be cut up but could go intact to the School
of Anatomy, a body being much more useful to the students
if nobody else had de-gutted it first. She would end her life
when she thought fit. It was her own.

But could she be free to 'think fit' while Harold was dodder-
ing around, requiring meals and sleeping-pills and clean
clothes: and a cup of tea at his lifelong haunt?

Jimmy Holly's chimney-corner was a much more literal
one, either, in winter, the stoke-hole of the greenhouse, or at
other times the log fire in the small sitting-room of the big
house, where the television flitted before uncomprehending
eyes. People who visited Jimmy Holly for his own sweet sake
were even fewer than those who dropped into Harold
Brandling's pet café to say how-do to an old image once
respected. Jimmy Holly had never been well known or
respected in rural life; he had retired before he became rural.

His visitors came on professional duty, not on duty dictated by kindness, as Harold Brandling's did. The parson: he
had to visit Jimmy Holly. It was not so bad when the sister
was around, but often she was busy in the kitchen or out
shopping, and then the parson had Jimmy to himself, a
daunting prospect. One could never guess whether Jimmy
understood *anything* that was said to him. A while before,
the parson had been shaken by the gift of a cheque for five
hundred pounds for some parochial nonsense, a cheque
readily honoured by Jimmy's bank. But it was so much too

L.F.—F

much that it rocked the parson on his heels. After that, he made his routine requests for donations to Janey, and received five pounds without the hundreds. Jimmy had been accustomed to shed large sums around in the days when he had possessed both the money and his wits. It was not apparent to outsiders when, exactly, he had begun to lose both those assets. Janey knew, and did her best to protect him.

The doctor visited Jimmy now and then from a sense of duty, because the old boy was old enough to be let off coming to the surgery, should there be anything wrong. There never was anything physically wrong. Blood-pressure, heart, chest, urine, all the items that could be sampled *in situ*, were fine. The doctor could do nothing for Jimmy's brain except ask to see the begonias or whatever, which always elicited pleasure and authentic-sounding information. Janey gave thanks for the doctor's visits; a kind and conscientious man he was, that was why he had chosen to be a GP instead of struggling into what were supposed to be the upper echelons simply because they had more money attached.

The doctor was in fact so kind and conscientious that he wished he could have a go at Janey, who was, as the young Radmere bobby had said, as thin as a wagtail trying to raise a cuckoo. But Janey was always 'fine' when asked, and never came near the surgery. You could not catch patients with bird-lime, even for their own good.

Another visitor was a fellow who would have remained at the back door or out in the garden in Jimmy's days of grandeur; a jobbing gardener who jobbed for half the village but not for Jimmy, and who had a special devotion to pot-plants. There had been a time when Jimmy had been very conscious of the class-barrier. But now he seemed even to have mastered Willie Stiff's Suffolk talk, in order to discuss delicate beauties and their special treatment. Janey had never been as conscious as Jimmy about back-door people and front-door people; she longed for Willie Stiff to come oftener, and if he had not had his own cottage and family, she would gladly have had him as a lodger in the too-large house: it would have been so interesting for Jimmy. It might have kept Jimmy's head alive for as long as his body seemed determined to live. Eighty-seven and quite idiotic about everything except pot-plants.

But, of course, still able, like a well-trained young child, to keep himself clean and do what he was told. The sister who was now his mother bade him change his clothes, have his bath, wash his hands, go to the lavatory. ('You know, Jimmy dear, you'll want to when we're down the street – or in the car – and there's no lav to go to.' If no response, 'You don't want to make me ashamed of you, do you, dear?')

This pathetic but necessary procedure would bring tears to Janey's eyes but not to Jimmy's. The big smile on the uncannily smooth face told her that no, he did not want to make her ashamed of him. And off he would stride, the powerful six-foot child, to the loo. In the midst of her responsibilities, Janey never failed to give thanks that Jimmy was nearly always a *good* child, and if ever he seemed less than gruntled, it was simply a case for syrup of figs.

The other oldie whom we have already met, Brigadier Gault, would have been furious to be called old. A man of seventy-four who kept himself in condition by digging his large garden, and playing bridge and taking an interest in politics for the sake of his mind, could not be called old. As for being looked after by his wife, *he* looked after *her*, trying to keep her from appearing a bigger fool than in fact she was. She was never let out without him except to go to the village shop across the Green. His chimney-corner was the vast carefully reconstructed fireplace, with dogs which could support half a tree between them, in his own house; and far beyond counting were the times when he had given poor Irene a dressing-down for, either with her own dustpan and brush or by orders to the washing-woman, causing the ash to be removed from the enormous grate. The fire never quite died in the ashes – it was a great waste to throw them out, as those who had tended the hearth in the 'hall' of a medieval great house well knew.

'But the dust, it blows everywhere with the wind down that huge chimney,' poor Irene would protest; she was brave enough to take one step in that direction.

'It's not dust, it's clean sterile ash, and anyway what are dusters for? You have the whole day to fill in somehow, Irene, you can dust *twice*, on a windy day.'

'It's so silly, to keep on doing work which could be avoided – '

'What *else* would you be doing, for God's sake? Woman's role in life is to do the needful repetitive jobs. Do you jib at making our bed every day?'

'That's different. I sleep in it and I like it to be aired and comfortable. Same with cooking, it's boring but I have to eat, all animals must, and it had better be eatable. For you as well as for me, both the bed-making and the cooking. But living in a thick layer of white ash or else doing the dusting twice a day – neither of those are *sensible*. Five minutes' clear-out and we get a clean hearth.'

'And you have thrown away a fine source of warmth, the hot glowing ashes which go on from week to week and month to month. We would never need to light this fire, if you did not throw out the living ashes – it would light itself.'

'Would you like to look after it yourself, just to make sure it does what you say?'

'Brraaach, no, the house is women's work,' said the Brigadier, and Irene, after an unusually long effort at making sense, gave up. His chimney-corner could accumulate an inch of white wood-ash, for all she cared. He could breathe wood-ash, eat wood-ash, if he enjoyed being a medieval manor-house owner. Perhaps it afforded him a recompense for his lost military command. Most of the things he did, his chess, his politics, his success with vegetables at the Radmere Hort. Soc., she regarded as substitutes for his lost military command. He would have been furious if he knew. But he could never have guessed. Irene having *critical* thoughts? What a laugh. Irene was a fool, like all women.

8
The Middle Years

Caroline Brandling, wife of Jonathan, was driving fast and competently to reach home in time to put lunch on the table, because Jonathan always came storming in for his food, which he seldom liked, and stormed out again in record time, so no wonder he had ulcers. Caroline had been to a coffee-morning at Castle Eyot in aid of something or other. It was not the Good Cause which had attracted her, but the certainty of finding a number of her friends there. All females, of course. The husbands were at work or at golf or made some other excuse: or else there weren't any husbands. Caroline was struck anew by the number of widows among her friends and acquaintances in the catchment area. At the coffee-morning there had been five from the Eyot itself, four from Radmere (and if the party had been held at Radmere there could have been a dozen) and three would have come from

Budgrave but for a recalcitrant motor-car.

'All of them of my generation,' thought Caroline. 'Mostly a bit older but certainly a younger bunch than my in-laws and their lot. What happened to all the husbands?'

And, 'Unless Jonathan lets up a bit, I'll soon be a widow too. Poor Jonathan, I wish he could be happier.'

The autumn landscape glowed all around in unaccustomed splendour, but for once Caroline was preoccupied with thoughts about her widowed friends. Two husbands had been claimed by World War Two, and a couple of others had been sent home from it too frail to live long, another had smoked himself into lung-cancer, a sixth had been knocked out in a matter of minutes by a heart-attack after mowing his lawn. Though without the facts about the rest, she had a strong impression that heart took the chief blame, with strokes and ulcers as runners-up.

All those men gone, in early middle age – the war victims even younger – and all their widows in their forties, fifties and sixties still going strong!

Why? Leaving out the freak storm of the late war, it was because the men worked themselves into a state (Jonathan certainly did) in order to maintain their wives and families, while the wives, though working when required to, as Caroline knew, did not have the responsibility.

She arrived at home and rapidly put pans on the electric stove and plates on the table in the dining-room. But the routine cooking for the light meal which was all Jonathan could face did not interrupt her train of thought.

'The wives demand too much,' she speculated, 'because there's been so much to be had, since the war. Old Pa-in-law, eighty-five, nobody asked too much of him. Ma had to manage without electric power until half-way through the war, no fridge, no washing machine, no freezer, no central heating, not even electric fires. What was there for wives to chivvy husbands *for*? But as soon as all that got going, most wives just nagged most husbands, gimme, gimme, gimme, to out-face other wives, and the husbands felt they had to boast to other husbands. And they died of it. Pa-in-law hasn't died because Ma demanded nothing. If anyone demanded, in that outfit, he did.

'But driving husbands to death seems to be only in our class. There aren't half as many widows per cent among our workers and all the other working people in the village. And that's a fact. Why?'

She strained and mashed the potatoes.

'Could be because there's a definite limit to wages and hours. The chaps can't kill themselves with overwork however much their wives nag. We farmers get cursed for paying low wages, and we'll have to pay more next year because of inflation but they'll still be low compared to what a glass-blower gets, ninety-nine pounds a week – and we produce food and you can't eat glass, so it does look cock-eyed. But Ma says it's better not to have a lot of money. Enough, she says. And it's not me that's pushed poor Jonathan into ulcers, and she knows it. We're friends, my mother-in-law and I.'

Jonathan burst in then, and stood by the table, very obviously controlling impatience, until all was laid before him. He then ate six mouthfuls, pushed his plate away and burst out again, leaving Caroline to her thoughts.

'It must have been the war that started it. He never says. Or coming home after all the stress and strain, to the old boy who was so awful to him that he had to go to sea again. No hope of a comfortable life at home – he was sent away under a Government scheme to learn farming under some other bloke who kept him making muck-heaps all the time. So the sea looked better – he was used to it. But the food was never a carefully-chosen diet.

'Then home again to me. And an ulcer op. which did no damn' good. And a long wait, losing money, till the old boy decided to make him manager, and at last partner. What's *wrong* with the old boy? Jealousy because Jon is Mamma's Other Man? Could be. Fathers hate their sons, I can get that much out of newspapers and *Reader's Digest*. And observation, which is worth twice as much: ask Ma-in-law.'

In the mid-afternoon, Jonathan gave up, came indoors, flung himself on the sofa in the sitting-room, and groaned. Caroline was ironing in the kitchen. Washing and ironing, coats and towels for the men in the milking-house as well as everything for her own household, occupied much of her time. Oh yes, many wives worked, in one capacity or another. But they did not pay the rent, the mortgage, the rates and taxes . . . they did not have the *responsibility*. Her mind was still on the same tack.

What will it be like to be a widow, because a widow I'll surely be? she asked herself. The ones I know are fine, jolly, putting on weight *and how*, busy if only going out to coffee-mornings and lectures and Bingo. How long did it take them to forget their husbands? To get used to the single bed? Some of them go home to dark and empty houses after their get-togethers. I'll be better than that. Jem will be back from college and working on the farm, and I doubt if Molly will rush away the moment she's done A-levels – I don't detect any passionate wish for independence. But a husband, taken for love, which means for good or ill: good *and* ill. There is good, it's not all ill, it's mixed. A husband's place can't be taken by children. They're sweet, mine are anyway, they're a comfort, but they're not Jonathan. I can still remember. All those good looks, all that charm, all those brains, God's gift to any girl (rich family and a thousand acres too, however far in the future). The only hidden thing was the ill health and the possible cause of it, the worrying nature. Oh, the changes since then. But nothing has changed the memories.

Meanwhile the other ladies of middle age (in a pretty wide sense) had also dispersed from the coffee-morning, some, like Caroline, to rush off in a car or on foot to produce a meal for husband and/or family, some, the lone ones, in no hurry at all. A woman by herself can do well enough on a boiled egg.

But there was a bunch of well-off widows who had arranged to have a pre-prandial drink a bit more stimulating than coffee and a lunch at the Castle Hotel, where they had lunched before, so they knew they could trust the food. These four gathered there had a lovely time discussing the other women at the coffee-morning. Not unkindly. Merely exchanging information and speculation. As Mrs Briscoe said, 'What's wrong with gossip? It keeps you in touch.'

Vera White said, 'Joan Weekes is beginning to pick up, she's twice the woman she was in every sense; I mean twice the weight, or nearly, and twice the conversation.'

'Poor thing, it can't have been any fun to watch Tim dying, with no hope and the knowledge that he's brought it on himself. I mean, she couldn't even curse God or the Government. No God or Government ever said that men must smoke forty or more cigarettes a day. It was a crushing experience for her – '

'And so long. An unconscionable time a-dying.'

'I can think,' said another of the friends, 'of some old dears who are an unconscionable time a-living. You know who I mean. That great house – '

Vera, the dominating personality, back-tracked to safety. 'Joan Weekes, don't you think, will have to give heed to her weight, now she has no more overwork and no more fear?'

'Unlike poor young Caroline Brandling, who still has overwork and fear. A sick husband is awful, you're so afraid of doing the wrong thing, and you get sworn at whatever you do. I know. I've had it. You stop even being sorry for him, because you're so sorry for yourself. And then he dies. And it lies on your soul like lead.'

'You know, there are clergymen and priests who say that pain and adversity clean up a person's character.'

'Obviously they haven't had any themselves,' said Vera White. 'Pain and adversity don't improve the character of the sufferer, why the hell should they? Nor the characters of the wife or daughter or other looker-afterer either, because with them it's complicated by fear of failing to do the medically proper thing. Poor cows, they might even *bring about* the death of their charges. As though it mattered! But it matters to them.'

'It mattered to you, Vera?'

'Not for long,' said Mrs White, who might have been a much younger sister of old Harriet Brandling. 'He'd had the life he chose, now I can have the life I choose, within the limits of my cash, and that's a bit narrow.' Mrs White was going to evening classes in Radmere to learn to be a potter. Her children were young grown-ups, but her pots were her infant children. She was happy. Her late husband, loved, pitied and in his extremity *feared*, was at peace. Never mind any speculations about an after-life, he was at peace and so was she.

Jessica Bray lived in half a cottage in the village of Cosgrave. It was not very comfortable because her only living-room was three-parts full of her grand piano. Besides this room she had a lean-to kitchen, a bedroom, use of bath-cum-loo which was not very tempting, and also use of the more attractive outside chemical closet. She had become adept at the wash-down in a basin of hot water which was, after all, what most people's grandmothers had had, gentles or simples, in country districts, before the dangerous practice

91

of laying on water into houses had become general.

Make the whole house damp, it would, and suppose the pipes leaked? And what happened to the – to the – cesspool? It would overflow in no time if people started having *baths*. East Anglia, devoid of flowing water, was very late in providing what many other parts, where water streamed down hillsides, already had. So Jessica Bray knew how to have a bath in a basin. One did not do it for fun, there was no splashing and snoozing in hot water, it was business and it was done properly. She planned to have a bath that evening. Meantime she put a casserole to heat in the oven and sat down at her piano.

She was not living absolutely alone, because the old couple who had rented half of the cottage to her were mostly at home. And she had her piano. No pianist was alone if there was a piano. But it could not report to the doctor if she should happen to break a leg or otherwise fall ill. It was sensible to have chosen a place however restricted where she could bang on the wall to communicate with a neighbour. She was not one of the affluent widows. Affluence had never come her way. It seldom came the way of a country parson. Now he was gone and she had a small pension and National Assistance, so she had not a wide choice of a place to live. But she did not repine. She made some extra money by acting locum for church organists, she played the piano – paid or not – at all kinds of functions, and she had many friends.

But Anne Skelton, who had had much difficulty in persuading herself to go to the coffee-morning, had no friends. She had money and a nice bungalow and that was all. That was all. She had become withdrawn when her marriage to a glamour-boy who wanted to live on her moderate riches came to an end when he found a richer patroness. Anne had to hide her failure, and she had not the wit or the talent to hide it behind any kind of accomplishment. She was not even a widow; the other woman, the second wife, was the widow when glamour-boy killed himself in a drunken car-crash. Anne was husbandless, childless and friendless. The house was always empty when she came back to it after shopping or any other excursion. There was not even a cat. There was, however, a lot of gin, to which Barry Skelton had introduced her.

That bloody coffee-morning! They had asked questions. 'Are you still living quite alone, Mrs Skelton? It's not a good idea.' She curled up and became a tight knot when people asked questions. True answers were humiliating. Lies, in her half-alive state, were difficult to substantiate. One forgot what one had said a week or a fortnight ago. The haunting fear was of being labelled dotty, because she could not keep up with what she had said or done even quite a short time before. Dotty meant being psychoed and then it might all come out: about the well-hidden gin. She could not manage this drab, deserted life without the support of the green bottle. Alcoholic? Heavens, no. She remained coherent and well able to drive her car, better able than half the new drivers who had passed their test last week. She was pretty sure no one would label her alcoholic unless first she had been labelled dotty because of some silly contradictions she had made in answering questions about her life, and why she chose to live alone. Without even a dog or cat. Apparently it seemed monstrous to women of her own age, with more or less her own resources in money. She could pay a companion, she could live in any one of a number of so-called hotels for the elderly – but she wasn't elderly, not yet fifty, and she did not want a companion who would ferret out the green bottles; and where, in any hotel or 'home', could she keep the green bottles from the notice of the domestic staff? She was all right in her bungalow with her bottles, as long as she resisted the temptation to go out to any kind of social 'do' where well-meaning women asked questions.

To herself, when herself asked questions, she had little to offer. 'I was a pudding-faced girl with some money from my dead father. I fell for *such* a pretty boy, and I was damned lucky when he found a richer woman because he'd just about run me dry. But oh, dear, such a pretty boy. Lovely to have about the place. I only divorced him because he begged me to, not because I wanted to. I'd have put up with anything, from him. I had no pride – what have I ever had to be proud about? *Only* that I'd captured him, and that was my money, not me. Now I've nothing except the bit of money he didn't squander.

'No, I'm not going out to any more coffee-mornings or any other places where I have to do more than ask across a counter for something I want; and all this self-service super-marketing is a great protection against having to speak.'

But because at her first appearance she had been a good spender at the bring-and-buy stall which accompanies any coffee-morning in aid of a good cause, many invitations came her way, and occasionally when she was feeling strong (that is to say after eleven o'clock in the morning) she was tempted by the hope that there might be someone who knew what total solitude was like, someone to talk to on equal terms. A friend. It never happened. The whole lot of them – they weren't always the same women, since the good causes were different – seemed to have *somebody*, if only a mongrel bitch, a stray, which had rewarded her befriender with five beautiful though peculiar pups. Glamour-boy had been afraid of dogs and allergic to cats. Anne Skelton therefore knew nothing about friendship with animals, the comfort of so many lonely people male and female. Before autumn shed its tears for winter, Anne Skelton was found dead in her garage, with a tube leading from the exhaust into the hermetically sealed body of the car. She had known how to fix her departure. Everyone who drives a car knows that. Enough petrol. A clean engine which will keep going. Shut all doors and all windows. Fix and tape the tube from the exhaust.

And Anne Skelton had no visitors, no visitors ever. So it worked. It was several days before the attention of the young policeman was alerted by a row of milk-bottles, one more each day, on the doorstep. He had a word with the milkman, who averred that Mrs Skelton had said nothing at all about going away, and that he himself was worried because the stalest of the bottles would have gone sour already. The young policeman was worried about something rather different. The Inspector ordered the house to be entered. Nothing there but a general lack of tidying-up. Then the garage. After the equivalent of two hundred miles, the petrol had run out and the engine was silent, but the driver had reached that bourne from which no traveller returns.

Anne Skelton provided an inquest for the two cub reporters, but a singularly dull one. No one knew anything about her. She had come fairly recently to live in the village of Cosgrave, she had no money problems, she had never consulted a doctor: these facts were easily unearthed by the police. Neighbours? No, she had never spoken to neighbours. Village shop? No, she had her own car in which she drove to Radmere or maybe Castle Eyot to do her shopping. The milkman had never seen her: she just left the money on the doorstep. No relative, no friend appeared in the Coroner's Court. The verdict was obvious, 'Suicide while the balance of the mind was disturbed.' Nobody had said anything about the balance of Mrs Skelton's mind, but to conclude that it was disturbed gave her a Christian burial.

'For what that's worth,' said Colin Crisp.

The two boys wrote identical reports because it was less trouble . . . Two women in the village, each reading a different report on publication-day, spoke quietly to one another. 'The pore thing, not even a cat nor a dawg.' 'The pore thing, nobody knowing she's gorn until owd Ted the milkman started worrying about the milk gooin' orf.'

'The pore 'oman, even a cat or a dawg 'd have held her to this world. But she never looked at the likes of us, *we* wasn't wanted. You can't shove in where you ain't wanted.'

'I wisht I had. Pore sould, I could croy for har.'

'She 'ouldn't want you to, Jessie.'

Caroline Brandling and her mother-in-law had read their newspapers. When next they met, as they often did, Caroline said, 'Wasn't it awful about that poor Mrs Skelton? I feel so *guilty*. I met her a couple of times, at coffee things, and I did try to talk to her because she stood about alone, but there was never anything but yes or no from her, she never said anything on her own, so I gave up. There must have been something we could have really spoken of, if I'd been more patient. But the papers say she didn't have a dog or a cat or even a bird. It was all silent, always, the neighbours and the postman and the milkman said.'

'Well, dear, no need for you to feel guilty; she evidently liked it like that.'

'But it's not natural. She must have been very unhappy.'

'To some, unhappiness is natural; they wouldn't know themselves without it – like the old girl and her petticoats, "Oh, deary deary me, this is none of I." It was probably Mrs Skelton's only claim to an identity.'

'But to choose to die, to die on purpose!'

'Not for you, not yet for me. We have our troubles but we cope. We don't opt out while we're still useful. What I guess about that poor woman is that she'd stopped being useful – if she ever had been.'

9
Also the Young

As well as being a catchment area for an appalling number
of the very old in all states of degeneration, Radmere caught
all the young of post-Primary School age. There was a good
Middle School for ages seven to eleven, which expanded
annually by means of prefabs, mobile classrooms and any
other enterprise offering a roof for the countless little kids
emerging from the area's Primary Schools. Every year, more
and more little kids. Well, you could understand it if you
went shopping in the narrow streets and were constantly
shoved off the pavements by twin-prams or near-twin prams
navigated by young mothers with two more little ones
running at heel. No one round this neck of the woods had
heard about overpopulation or birth-control; East Anglia
was always a day behind the fair. For example it had been,
years before, the last county to adopt the Burnham Scale for
teachers' pay, and now in 1975 it had its face stonily set

against Comprehensive schooling and only at the last moment, under threats from above, had done away with the ludicrous eleven-plus exam.

Besides the Middle School, bursting out of its doors, there was a messy though efficient Grammar School built in 1908, most of its surrounding land covered with later buildings, canteen, laboratories, Assembly-cum-theatre, you name modern requirements, Radmere Grammar had them – only, it had had to remove its playing-fields to the outer edge of town because those fields originally donated had been built over; and also there was a two-part (half boys, half girls) Secondary Modern School of much later design and in far more playing-acres, about half a mile away from the Grammar.

These post-eleven schools became filled to bursting by the recent decree that all children, even those who disliked, despised or were impervious to education, must remain at school until the age of sixteen. And now in 1975 another disaster-course was set. For with the long-delayed abolition of the eleven-plus exam, which nobody loved because it had been proved to occur too early in a child's career, came a directive from on high (the County) that the parents were to choose the schools for their children. And in the catchment area ninety-five per cent of parents, for prestige reasons which might have meant something fifty years earlier but were now old hat (not that East Anglia was ever sensitive about being behind the times) opted for Grammar School.

Regardless of any recommendation from the Middle School staff, regardless of the inevitable overcrowding and understaffing, regardless of anything but the now outdated social lift of 'gooing to Grammar', the parents made their purblind choice. Many of those parents had themselves failed to get to Grammar, and now that there was no more failing, now that failure was no longer in the dictionary, their children must have the class-label of Grammar as of right.

There were loud wailings in the staff-room at the Grammar.

'We've no *room*. We've had no room for more than a year.'

'The leavers from this school are so few, they mostly want to stay to get to university, and there's this flood of God-knows-what coming in. We've no *room*.'

'And no time on the time-table,' said the young man who helped the Head with this nigh-insuperable task. Neither of them could see how a computer would manage better; computers had to be fed with information by mere human beings.

The most frightened and most vocal was the art-master, and with good reason. He had come to know, from earlier experience in 'the other school', that about eighty per cent of the new overwhelming intake would be arty-and-crafty kids, however ham-handed, rather than academics. They would be children for whom the Secondary Modern Schools had been purposely designed, children who could be happy and productive there, but who had been misdirected by their parents' outdated social ideas. In any society, a bare twenty per cent was academic, in either of the two disciplines, Arts or Sciences; the rest were doers who ought to be encouraged to do, even if the doing were only ploughing, hoeing and harrowing.

Stephen Post was more desperate than the rest for three reasons: he was the one and only art master at the Grammar: he was very keen on his work: he did not know how he could possibly cope with the huge prospective intake.

'We must have more staff. An all-ability school needs a staff to teach all abilities. Not just the clever ones and leave the rest helpless. This is a school for the clever ones, and we're going to get the stupes as well because their pig-ignorant parents can *choose*. And look at the Sec. Mod. School, it's going to be half empty. Bloody lunatics, our Masters. Doing away with that rotten exam, OK, but putting nothing in its place.'

'Well, what?'

'You know. Integrate the schools into a Comprehensive.'

'But the other one's half a mile away.'

'What's half a mile on a bike? Five minutes and fine 'em if they're late. This school could be the Maths and Science, in the widest sense, including Geography, and Domestic Science which gets more scientific every day, because we have the best labs. The Other School could be Literature, Languages, Arts and Crafts, with a bit of come and go when necessary – '

'Where does history come in?' asked a middle-aged and learned woman who taught it.

'History is literature, a lot of it fiction,' said Stephen Post, lean, dark and thoroughly worked-up. 'The undeniable facts, dates, battles, kings, are very few, the rest is speculation coloured by politics. History would go into the literary package in the Other School, for the bright ones. The less bright will be learning how to write what they mean.'

'Isn't that the function of Grammar,' said the learned lady, 'to teach them to write or say what they mean?'

'Not for the science lot. Science has gone into fantasy. Far beyond grammar and syntax. They make up words and symbols and stick them down anyhow. My job, teaching kids to see and paint, is much more like literature, teaching them to read and write. I'd be at the Other School, you could call it the Arts school.'

'You mean integration. Grammar and Mod. in one. A Comprehensive. But there's half a mile between the two and a lot of truancy can happen in half a mile.'

'So what? If they don't want to learn, they'll run off. Let 'em. If they care, they'll pop back and forth, when they have to, in five minutes.'

Precisely the same problems – no room at the Grammar and that half-mile between the schools – activated the more realistic of the minds at the Governors' Meeting towards the end of that summer term, the frightening influx of all and sundry in September being definitely expected. The Governors were local worthies without any powers. They might offer advice, but no more.

An old wrinkled woman governor made herself heard by dint of a powerful voice: 'You could integrate the schools by looking at the older universities. The students walk or bike far more than half a mile to their lectures and tutorials, and make no bones about it, if they want to learn. I played truant if I was bored, but the boredom lay at the teacher's door.'

'It's a different generation now,' said the Secretary from the County Education Committee.

'Young man,' said the old girl (the Secretary was at least forty), 'even the children of today have brains of a sort, unless they are ESN. Half a mile of by-road should not be thought an insuperable barrier to education. If we must take this large mixed lot on the say-so of their ignorant parents, then we must go Comprehensive in order to have double the premises, double the staff and double the playing-space. Stands to reason. We must have room for all these young things and we must have a large staff. And *they*, the kids and the staff, would be the better of plenty of space for games. I can't see the objection. The Other School – more modern and better designed than this, I may say, and with acres of ground – is, after all, a place of secondary education, not a reformatory or an Infant School or a Special School or anything we couldn't adjust to.'

'The parents,' said the Headmaster, 'wish their children to go to Grammar School.'

In the sixth-form common-room, the head boy and head girl

were jointly holding a meeting.

'Look, all of you,' said Tom Sanford, 'Janice and I have been bidden to attend the Staff Meeting tomorrow. What's it mean?'

'Student Power,' suggested a big spectacled boy.

'Not power, more likely student help,' said Janice White. 'If you know anything about anything, George, which I often doubt, you'll know that at least a hundred and fifty allsorts are being pushed in here next term by their parents, because the exam has gone. And how many of us are leaving? Perhaps ten. There's no room and no staff for the allsorts. If you ask me, Old Grey Boss is worried sick, Steve Post too.'

'Well, we can't help,' said a lanky girl. 'We've got our own work to think of, we're all on A-levels. You don't get *me* volunteering for a pupil-teacher to keep the brats quiet.'

'I don't think that's why Tom and I have been bidden to Staff Meeting, but I wish I did know why,' said Janice.

Spectacled George weighed in again. 'Maybe the old sod's wakened up at last. He's always pretended not to know that most of us in the Sixth will be voters next year, and able to get married and get mortgages and get killed for our country if there's a war and if we aren't smart enough to shoot our big toes off – '

'Oh, shut up, George, or keep to the point,' said Sanford the convener. 'Anyone got any questions, or better still instructions for Janice and me?' He winked at Janice and she winked back. Ninety-six per cent at the Grammar School, including most of the staff, would have said 'for Janice and I', but Sanford, Modern Languages, and Janice, Eng. Lang. and Lit., were perfectionists.

A first-year Sixth spoke up. 'Do we have to take this lot regardless?'

'It's Parents' Choice,' explained Sanford. 'Brains don't

count any more, only Parents' Choice. There no exam in case some little tots should have to fail: failure's *out*. And it could be OK, you know, like Eton, if we had twice the room and twice the staff. But we haven't. It's not yet like Eton.'

'And we're stuck with it.'

'Seems so, that's what's driving the staff up the walls.'

'There might be twenty leaving,' a girl suggested. 'I know four in the Fifth. Two girls who want to be hairdressers – '

Snorts and laughter. 'Never ought to have been here at all. The eleven-plus was pretty elastic. No crowds then, so minimal literacy and you were in. The eleven-plus is no loss,' said Sanford, 'but Parents' Choice is worse. We'll get lots and lots of hairdressers and dozens more with no ambitions whatsoever.'

'Except boy-friends – *and* girl-friends,' said Janice. 'It's not only the girls who are unacademic.'

'Anyway,' said Sanford, 'twenty or thirty leaving, if we could hope for so many, are nothing to the flood that's coming in. What I want to know is, does the invitation to Staff Meeting mean that we just have to listen, or are we expected to produce ideas? Anybody got any ideas?'

Spectacled George said, 'Firstly we ought to attend the Govs' Meetings too – '

'That's not an idea, it's a bee in your bonnet. And nothing to do with the matter now before the meeting,' said Janice.

'Besides, old fire-eating Gault would probably shoot anyone representing the mere pupils,' said someone.

George said, 'You're out of date. He's been sacked, the polite way is "compulsorily retired", under the age limit. My uncle, Harry Elwood, is all in favour of student participation.'

'Oh, *him*,' said Sanford dismissively. 'Could we get back to the point? Anybody know what can be done with the coming influx of mothers' darlings?'

'Shift all the lower forms off to the Other School. Make it a Junior Grammar.'

'And what about the kids already *at* the Other School?'

'What about them? They're on speaking terms with our kids, I hope. And there'll be a lot of room there, with all their sixteens leaving, and nobody, but nobody, going in.'

Sanford sorted out these offerings and said, 'There's an idea at last. A place where there's room.'

A tall sourfaced girl said, 'You know what you're saying. Mixing Them and Us is "Going Comprehensive".'

'We might have to, at that. A simple matter of logistics, if you know what that means.'

'I also know we haven't got the staff for it,' said the sour girl.

'Plenty of staff for the lower forms at the Other School already,' said Janice.

'You try selling that to Old Grey Boss,' said the girl. 'I wouldn't be in your shoes. Comprehensive is his dirtiest word.'

'Because it's the County's too, no doubt,' said Sanford. 'Can't say I fancy it myself for the Fifth and Sixth, but Jan says that's only prejudice. Well, anyway, about this Staff Meeting. Maybe Jan and I won't have to open our mouths, maybe we'll just be *told* what's on. But if we have to utter, we can. Thank you very much, ladies and gents, meeting over.'

In the event, the head boy and head girl were indeed told, not asked. And their function was to explain and smooth over decisions already made by Old Grey Boss. He had this name because, though not very old, he had a thick grey thatch so neatly fitting that bets were laid about its being a wig (but it had never been seen even slightly askew) and also cold grey eyes and always grey clothes, a hangover from his teaching days when grey had accepted chalk-dust better than darker colours. In summer he exchanged grey tweed for grey linen jacket and grey flannel bags. His complexion was somewhat olive, which made the cold grey eyes very noticeable.

He started with Sanford and Janice.

'You two are here because if anybody among the pupils is trustworthy and serious-minded, it ought to be the Sixth Form, since you have your own interests at heart as well as those of the school. You need to do well, because it's now or never. I take it you are aware of the difficulties we shall have next term, with almost every eleven-year-old being sent here by its parents. I'll tell you what has been decided, and it will be your job to explain and in a sense police the plan.

'We shall need the sixth-form common-room for a class-room, also the library, except for an hour on Fridays at the end of school for the exchange of books. In addition there will have to be what they call mobile classrooms, Heaven help us, on the hard tennis court. I know it's the only sizeable playing-space near to the school, and the only hard court we have. But there's no choice except Parents' Choice, so we have to submit.

'You seniors, the Fifth and Sixth, will betake yourselves to the Other School for much of your time. You will find good common-rooms, space for your work-books from our own library, peace and quiet for the large amount of work you do on your own, a good canteen, and at least five tennis courts both hard and grass and plenty of other games-space. The scientists among you who need to come here for the labs, and anyone for other special teaching, will mount bicycles and take not more than five minutes in transit. Those who come to school by bus and have no bicycles will *run*. This will break you in, you must realize, for university life. It is not at every university that you find all your needs grouped round a campus. The policing will come when you two,

Sanford and Janice, appoint bicycle-monitors. That is the outline of the plan. Any questions?'

Janice was afraid of nobody because she was a female and females had to stand up for themselves *or else*. She said,

'It would have been simpler to send all the lower forms to the Other School, keeping Four, Five and Six here because of labs and the library. The staff could do the commuting because they have cars. They could do the trip in two minutes, not five. And there's heaps of room along there for mobile classrooms without taking up our only hard court. Didn't that occur to anybody – Sir?'

'It would have been *integration*,' said the Head, as though the word smelt. 'You have to remember that about half the Secondary Modern pupils will still be there, and to put our juniors in with them would be to create an integrated Junior School. We must somehow, however great the difficulty, keep the Grammar School separate. That, after all, is what the parents want, though at least sixty per cent are misguided. Their little dears are to come to a Grammar School, and the ones to be displaced to make room for them are our seniors, who can best understand the problem.'

'It's idiotic, to me,' said Janice. 'Sir.'

'The parents are idiotic to me, girl, though don't quote me on this. They are our masters now though most of them can't tell a hawk from a handsaw. Explain, as the exam-papers say.'

'Harnser, sir. A heron.'

'Right. Well. The parents want their brats to come to this ugly conglomeration of buildings with its playing-fields away down the road because its name is Grammar School. And what they want they must have. The decree has gone forth.'

'And we have to fit in somehow,' said Sanford.

'Just so. And the people I can trust to make the best of

it, in their own interest as well as the school's, are naturally my seniors. And don't lose sight of those abundant tennis courts.'

He held them with his ice-grey eyes. They could not instantly reply, so he finished: 'And when we come to think of it, we ought not to be surprised or angry at the choice made by all these parents, however unsuitable in some cases. It is a compliment. It is because we – the staff, the senior pupils, and myself – have given this place a good reputation: not only in learning, I like to think, but in responsible, polite, considerate behaviour. This is what I am asking of us all, and believe me, I'm included, in the present *impasse*.'

After that, who could protest? Certainly not the staff, who were in a worse position than the pupils when it came to protesting. The staff were paid minions of the County who could be sacked. The pupils were not paid, merely subsidised; and State school pupils had far less idea of the source of the money for their education than had those whose parents groaningly paid fat fees for them at 'Public Schools'. More-over, no State school pupil could be sacked except for grossest crime such as being drunk or drugged on school premises; and even then, the State had to continue his education somewhere else, because the State was bound to see that every child of every class, every child however sinful and however dumb, had an education up to the age of (at least) sixteen. The position of a young person at school, whether he did well or ill, was far more secure than that of anybody else in Britain: which gave him, perhaps, a false confidence when he came to be in receipt of *pay*.

The Staff Meeting ground to a halt, and Sanford and Janice went off to collaborate on their report to their contemporaries.

'George will be the snag.'

'George is always the snag. Is it Ego or moral or political

conviction? If I thought it was conviction I could give him
rope – '

'It's not moral conviction, anyway; he hasn't any morals.
I should know,' said Janice. 'And I don't think politics
should rear their ugly heads so early in our lives.'

'You and I can both vote, you know.'

'I know. But putting a cross at an election isn't the same
as political thinking, not at our age anyway.'

'I sometimes feel a hundred.'

'Poor love, so do I sometimes but I damn' well know I've
another A-level to get before I can go to university. And so
have you. If we'd done a shade better, we'd have left this
bedlam to the next in succession – '

'To George, God help them all.'

Sanford and Janice hoped to rectify their educational
omissions before Christmas. The next in succession was
disgruntled, brainy, thoroughly awful George with his
notions about student power. Both Sanford and Janice had
a proper reverence for learning, and could not see any
connection with power except perhaps in its very highest
ranks; among those in possession of vitally important and
absolutely undeniable facts. And where were the undeniable
facts? Facts in 1970 were different from facts in 1980, and
after the year 2000, who knew what the facts would be? The
only power conferred by study, and only to a very few students
at that, Janice often said to George, was the power to say or
write exactly what they meant: and even that was no great
shakes unless what they meant was good sense in the first
place.

When they reported to the Sixth in their small and crowded
common-room, George's instant reaction was predictable.

'We'll go on strike.'

'And what good would that do? We two need to work all
the time we have, if you don't,' said Sanford.

'Use your loaf,' said George. 'A sit-in strike. Then they can't use either this room or the library as classrooms. We'll call out the Fifth as well, and sit in both places.'

'And sing "We shall not be moved",' said Janice.

'OK, and get on with our bloody work as well, since you're so keen on it.'

'Without any teaching?'

'You two can do without teachers for a week; by that time the Establishment will have torn its hair out and got four mobile classrooms instead of two, and the rest of us who aren't crazy about work will have had an extended summer holiday and a sing-song. A couple of record-players, and we could have two nice discos going.'

'Oh, George, you are an ass.'

'They do it at universities, there's always a sit-in going on at one or another. You'll be sitting-in when you get there – '

'Not in our last year, with Finals coming up,' said Sanford, 'which is more or less the position we're in here at this moment. Come to that, half the Sixth is in its last year, and Janice and I will be going after one term if we manage to fill up our A's. Don't you understand about work, George? You've a second year in the Sixth, I know, but it's time you got wise. If you don't do reasonably well, it'll affect your whole life.'

'Listen to the Reverend,' snorted George. 'I am looked after from the cradle to the grave, bor, whether I go on strike or not, whether I ever do any work or not. Whether I ever get a bloody A-level or not. And so are you. So why sweat? I'll tell you; swank, prestige, look at my brains. That's you. I reckon I'll be getting more money than you, three times as much, when I get to the point of chatting up a real nice bird with the idea of a home and a fam'ly.'

Sanford lost his patience. 'Then why in Hell are you at Grammar School? How did you get here at all? Why didn't you quit at sixteen to go and sweep out a factory? Why are you wasting taxpayers' money by two years in the Sixth?'

'Because I've brains, laddie, though not your sort. I've discovered a secret you haven't. *Otium cum diggin' a tatie*, some old comic called it. In this blest twentieth century, we only need to be alive. We only need to watch out for death. Look both ways when you cross the road, you and Janice.'

10
More Education

'But, Mr Howlett,' said George who lived in the next village and was aware of the pre-retirement identity of the ex-shop-steward, Mr Howlett, the neighbour of Brigadier Gault. Mr Howlett had registered in George's mind, as an adult supporter of student power. But it seemed that George had been mistaken.

'See here, boy, George isn't it?' said Howlett, 'who pays for your schooling? I do, among others. You have no right, while you are being kept, nor have stupid university under-grads on grants from public money, to go on strike or mess up other kids' education in any way. *You have no right.* The right may come when you stop being paid for. If you ever do.'

'But, Mr Howlett, you've called a lot of strikes yourself.'

'And who were my strikers? Men who earned wages and maintained homes and families. Not school-kids in receipt of

public subsidy, you goof, paid out in taxes by me and those
of my mates who earned enough to be taxed. It's not only
millionaires who get taxed, you know. Not only the Upper
Class, millionaires or not. The rich men have to pay more
because they can, but people like me have to pay too, as
much as we can. And kids like you, George, pay nix, you
are takers, not payers, and unless you work bloody hard at
school you never will be payers, you'll be takers all your lives.
That could be what you want, but to me it stinks. You're not
in my league, young George. Go away and forget your silly
strike. The educational mess will settle itself in two or three
years, and during that time you ought, if you've any brains
at all, to move on to some college or other and get a qualifica-
tion for *work*, George, work and wages, without which you're
a ghost, a nobody in my book,' said Mr Howlett.

'The generation gap,' muttered George. Howlett still
believed in and respected earning-capacity: George didn't:
he didn't have to: you could sit on your fat bum as long as
you could find any excuse for doing so, redundancy, physical
illness, psychological difficulties, you name it, George knew
about it, and you would have social services augmented by
all sorts of do-gooders looking after you, you poor dear
thing. Opposition to Society enlisted various funnies on your
side, their emotions stronger than their brains, but who would
quarrel with that?

Howlett was a disappointment. George had hoped to
produce him as a man of the industrial and economic world
who would back the Grammar School strike at least by
letters to the Press. He knew of no other adult likely to be
interested. And Howlett had proved to be of the wrong
generation. So few people of the right generation were old
enough to carry any weight. It was awful to have to admit
that only the old and the middle-aged *knew* anything about
Life – and what they knew was at odds with what the young

wanted them to know. Only the young could understand the young – but could they understand anything else? The world had been hobbling along for a hell of a time. Even George knew that he was only born yesterday. It was his one concession to twentieth-century life. Anyone could find out from his birth-certificate that he had missed an awful lot of history.

But history was past. George was for the future. His trouble was, he couldn't find anyone else in the Radmere catchment area who had his political slant about the future. They just were not with it. Howlett had been his big hope, but Howlett, after all, was a retired man. Going to his grave. The wrong generation.

And even his own generation, Sanford and Janice for instance, had not freed itself from Howlett's preoccupation with work and wages. Work and wages, or at any rate stamps in your book to entitle you to Unemployment Benefit, were respectable. But why? Why not *no* work, the dolce vita, a fishing rod, a dollygirl, and *no* wages, just the most the State would give you because you had been born into it? That was what the Proletariat had been working for from the year dot: the right to live. To live without working, without kowtowing, without doing any bloody thing, if that was how you wanted it, but living and eating under some sort of watertight roof. Basic human rights. Because you were born a human child.

Janice and Sanford sometimes wondered whether George had been born a human child. It depended on whether you thought Caliban was human or not.

'Do you think George really means to live his whole life on Social Security like he says?' asked Janice.

'Depends what sort of girl-friend he gets. It's you women who want everything "done proper",' said Sanford.

'I can't see any girl taking up with George. I mean, look

round our age-group in this school: who'd have him?'

'Any girl who didn't want to work for her own living; either too lazy or not bright enough. Ought not to be at this school, you could say. But there *are* some, got in as kids when the pressure was less and the eleven-plus could be elasticated a bit.'

'That would mean George marrying a Georgina, and *both* on Social Security, not to mention their kids. And us being taxed for them – '

'And now that even the eleven-plus has gone, it will happen over and over again, *in Grammar Schools*, that people with no ambition and no brains – George does have some brains, of a sort – will link up and produce another generation with no ambition and no brains, happy as Larry to live on other people's taxes . . . When you think, Jan, the hard work you and I put in to get here, and to stay here, and to move on to where we're moving on to, well – '

'After us, the deluge. There'll be no point in having brains or working hard any more.'

'And no point in Grammar Schools any more,' said Sanford with extreme melancholy, which anyone who knew his background, as Janice did, could understand. His step up, at the age of eleven, from farm-working life into the embryo professional class had been hard-won and decisive. His family had been proud of him. There would be no call for pride any more, when a kid 'went to Grammar' on its parents' say-so. Sanford had justified every confidence which anybody had had in him: a good solid intelligent lad, not yet stretched to his full ability: strong in health, to sustain hard work and an active brain. He was one of the best lads, his current Head thought (though without much knowledge of other good post-1908 boys – it wasn't like some historic Grammar School) who had passed into these local groves of academe.

The sad thing was, Sanford was not madly proud of himself, but he was proud of his school. And he saw it foundering in the general mud of late-twentieth-century education, when even mere literacy didn't matter. You didn't have to spell, or use logical grammar, or the right dictionary words. Without any of those, you got to be a journalist or even a talking face on the telly. You could earn real lolly, you could have a nest for your bird and your chicks, without even trying – knowing bloody nothing, by the standards of Sanford, who had had to acquire knowledge.

Janice, who had known him and loved him since they both arrived at Grammar School, though her background was different (the family of a dedicated Socialist doctor who felt that if the State had not yet got around to educating scientists it was about time), understood Sanford's pride in achievement. She had had to weather some storms, because she was not a scientist, medical or any other kind. She, like Sanford, was a literary cuss. Words, in a variety of languages, were their science. And could anybody say – seeing what staggering misunderstandings arose from misuse of words – that the proper use was not a science? Both Janice and Sanford (who possibly did not know that she had marked him for her own) had had their battles in order to arrive at the kind of school they needed. And now?

'Look,' said Janice, 'if the two schools in this town could be properly integrated into a Comprehensive, with the great big staff, more than just the two joined together, which would be wanted, we needn't feel we've lost our school. There would be the university streams both arts and sciences, and the tech. streams, and the commercial and practical streams and nobody spitting at anybody else, that's the ideal, isn't it, and it could come to life *here*, given time. Meanwhile you and I will be long gone, the lucky ones who got away before the strife.'

'But a Grammar School won't be a Grammar School any more.'

'It isn't now, Sandy. You and I aren't made to learn Greek and Latin, the basis of grammar. How much grammar do you know? Bloody little, like me. Not only don't we know Greek or Latin, we don't know English. Can you do parsing or analysis? I'm weak on them, I only know they exist because of my pa and ma. According to them, I talk and write nonsense, and so of course do you. Because the Grammar School does not teach grammar. And you know, love, however much you know about other things, you can't get a word of it across accurately without grammar. You and I are hellish lucky to be going on to places where we may learn something. Don't get a hang-up on Grammar Schools, Sandy, they've had it. They aren't special any more.'

'We are the end of an era?'

'Seems like. Of course there'll be a new era if ever the free schools get together into something like the pay-schools, all-abilities and squads of staff so that everyone gets a chance. My mother went to one of those, my father too – it was more usual for boys. The Public School was an all-ability school; you got into it, if you hadn't any brains, by either having a lot of money or being the son of an old boy. Anyway you got in.'

'Like this school now. You get in. The reasons are even flimsier, but you get in. I'm glad I'm getting out.'

In the village of Pye, a stubby dark lad of eleven was holding forth in his parents' kitchen.

'I ain't a-gooin' to Grammar. I don' wanna goo to Grammar. Dick Spink he ain't only one year older'n me and he goo to the Other School and he loike that, he whoolly do. He git on well there, he'd look arter me.'

Bill Dark's dad, a tractor-driver, an older and heftier

version of his son, said, 'You'll goo to Grammar.'

'Whoy?'

'Becorse I say so.'

'Did you goo to Grammar, Pa?'

'Never had the chanst. That's whoy you hafta. You got the chanst. The fust one of our fambly to hev the chanst.'

Bill Dark had four elders, three brothers and a sister, one brother in jail, one emigrated, one in the Army, the sister at the Other School, very happy and learning to cook like anyone's dream-girl. A typical family of the non-academic kind. Bill was the youngest: and at long last it had become possible for his parents, regardless of Bill's mental rating, to send him to Grammar.

'You can't make me goo.'

'I s'll take you in moy car, never moind toime orf from wukk,' said his father. The mother had a fridge and a washing-machine, the father had a car; what they didn't have was any education, any faintest notion of fundamental logic, let alone literature, science or art. Dimly they knew their lack, which the youngest boy might fill. He might get into a bank or Local Government, no less. Father and Mother had no means of knowing the unteachableness of their youngest – they had been unteachable themselves. They only knew this was a chance of Grammar School chucked into their laps.

Pa Dark drove Bill to the Grammar School. Bill saw him drive away and hared the half-mile to the Other School, where his one-year-older sister took charge and booked him in, just as he had hoped. No trouble about shortage of room. Bill was in. And happy. Put a pencil in Bill's hand and he could draw a tractor or a tree, a baler or a barn, and in the first days of term while things were settling down, nobody asked him to do anything else. His parents knew so little about schools that with the co-operation of his very slightly older sister they remained in the comfortable belief that he was at Grammar. They pushed him on to the bus every morning, and the two arrived not quite together every evening.

The parents had done their duty: they had demanded Grammar for a son as soon as it became possible to do so.

And young Bill had done his duty too: he had stood out for the companionship of his friend and his sister and the school which, he had been told, was a good place for them.

Others were not so lucky. Bill, though un-intellectual, was highly intelligent. Many other non-intellectuals, that September, were pushed into Grammar by parental ambition – and lost, lost for ever. Only Steve Post's art-classes gave them brief respites, since art is for everybody. The rest of their time they were swimming in an adverse current. For they were at a Grammar School, where literacy was expected. However lax the modern 'grammar' education, you had to be able to read, to make any sense of it at all: to read and to count. In modern jargon, you had to have literacy and numeracy (who invented that one?) and many of the little elevens pushed into Grammar School by ambitious Mas and Pas had neither, so various were the village schools from which they came. Some schools managed to teach the three Rs, among finger-painting, nature-study and home-made drama, some just kept the kids quiet.

September was a shambles. September 1975.

A date to remember in this the most backward province of Britain; a date when parents could opt to send their offspring, however bright or ESN, to Grammar School, regardless of suitability – regardless of anything but parental hopes of social climbing. The mess could have been, bit by bit, arranged, had the County bosses gone all out, earlier, in favour of fixing up Comprehensive Schools in each of their huge catchment areas, and had been able to face the expense of staffing such schools. But to most of the Education Committee, 'comprehensive' was anathema – and the

County, always a reluctant spender, was glad of the excuse of the Government's current economy drive: nothing, but nothing, could be done for education except a cutting-down of such frills as evening classes. It saved a lot of thinking. No steps forward were called for, only steps back.

This was the essence of staff-room talk at Radmere. The staff-room looked out upon the ex-hard tennis court, now a tennis court no longer. The view from the staff-room window was straight into the side of one of the mobile classrooms. There was no room for tennis now, close to the school; only two rather poor grass courts on the official playing-field down the road. The town club, with good courts, liked a young entry and charged little; but there again, one could not grab a racket, an opponent and a couple of balls and rush out for a valuable ten minutes' practice on the backhand. An amenity especially enjoyed by the seniors had been lost.

But there were courts and courts and courts, far from fully used, at the Other School. This was one of the reasons why George's sit-in strike did not happen. On mature reflection, the Fifth and Sixth decided that they would not be at all ill-done-by at the Other School. George fairly foamed at the mouth:

'Bloody *tennis*. You'll forget your principles for a lousy *game*. We are Grammar School, and the only proper alternative is a Comprehensive. Don't you see, we'll never get a Comprehensive system while they can push us around like this, and we don't get a Grammar School either. Neither fish, flesh, fowl nor good red herring, that's us. You stinking spineless lot. You could *compel* Them to think of something, just by sitting on your fannies. And why won't you? Games, idiot lunatic games!'

'Finished, George?' said Sanford, presiding for the last time over a senior meeting, not in their old common-room

119

but out of doors on the staff car-park, so complete was the displacement.

'Too right, I'm finished,' said George. 'I quit. Find me if you can and if you want to. I don't care if I never see any of you lot again, you sloppy weak-kneed tripe-hounds.'

Later, Janice said to Sanford, 'He'll be all right, you know. He has as much brain as any of us and more gab than most. He'll turn up on telly, you wait.'

'I hope so,' said Sanford. 'It 'ud make a nice change. Was the bloody Box ever worse than in this summer just departing? If there's one ambition I do not have, however big the money, it's to make a cockshy of myself on telly. Acting in proper plays is something else: but being one's silly self answering bloody silly questions, damned impertinent as often as not, or else so stupid that they can't be answered at all (why the hell don't interviewers get trained and have to pass an exam?), that's not me, I have no ambitions that way. George is welcome, if you're right. Me I want to go to university and learn a lot more than I know now, which isn't much. What about you, Jan?'

'Same. The more I learn, the more I find I don't know. That's education in a nutshell.'

'No, love, only in the upper reaches. The others get a couple of O-levels and think they know it all.'

Janice thought for some long moments, then said, 'You know, Sandy, George is right. This huge wave of little kids; some of them are Grammar kids and all of them are too young, anyway, to be sorted into sheep and goats. They want a great big school with a gi-normous staff to give them all a good kick off. Some of the most backward might just have had bad teaching or silly parents. George is right about the Comprehensive bit. It's a pity he's so awful. He won't get anywhere, will he, he won't even last long on the Box, unless he can learn to be less awful.'

'Abrasive is the word,' said Sanford. 'Gets on everybody's wick.'

'Well, can one be highly intelligent *and* dedicated to a Cause, any Cause, without getting on everybody's wick?' asked Janice. 'When you say "everybody" you have to include hundreds of thousands who can't even get their minds to work. The only things they don't find abrasive are football and the Miss England competitions. Games and girls. The great silent majority are like that.'

'And, God help us, they all have votes,' said Sanford.

11
The Press

After the Gault-Howlett case the summer had dragged for
the apprentice reporters of the two strictly local papers.
They both might have been seen, about once a week on
different days, circulating Willington Green on their bicycles,
and hopping off to chat to any ancient who might be found
toddling to his mid-day pint. And always the reporter was
disappointed. There had been no more shooting during
prohibited hours, nor had the thatched house been burnt
down. A pity. The ancients seemed to have forgotten the
whole affair, as had the reading public. Summer was a
flat time. The big news was the lovely sunshine which soon
became the damned frightful drought. Neither of the reporters knew anything about farming or gardening, they
only knew a very little about nouns and verbs and how to
spell – well, they didn't know much about proper names or
names of places, they just hoped. Farming and gardening were

important and had specialist writers in both papers. The reporters had to go back to the grind of weddings, funerals, and the occasional (seldom fatal, alas) road accident: they could just pray to get their spelling right. They often didn't.

The peculiar rearrangement at the senior schools in Radmere was a blessing to both reporters, whose editors had been harrying them. They were sent out on a definite assignment, in the second week of September.

One of the papers was supported by the County daily, of liberal tradition since the year dot; the other was privately owned by the truest blues. So the official views on the school mess-up were divergent, except on the point that there *was* a mess-up.

Caused by? The true-blue said by the abolition of the eleven-plus exam. The rosier paper said by not making proper Comprehensive provision before this abolition.

The really poignant side-issue was that the true-blue reporter was red as roses in his personal beliefs, while the other lad was somewhat, though not so strongly, the other way. Each boy was reduced to being a mere recorder of what to the best of his knowledge was fact (and the best of his knowledge was not very good). No opinion, no feeling could come into his reporting, any more than into the reported weddings and funerals of total strangers. What they reported was not supposed to be of any personal interest to them. When you left school at sixteen-plus with a couple of O-levels related, though not very closely, to grammar and spelling, you jolly well took what offered, and throttled your ambition, your conscience, your religious or political convictions, your hopes of heaven. What you had to have was a salary, however small, to make you partly, at least, independent of your bullying he-man dad and your smothering mum. Enough to take a bird out for a drink and a disco, and save up for a parka and that far-distant motor-bike. You went on living with ghastly Dad and Mum of course because it was cheap: Mum was content with two quid a week, and where else could you get grub and washing for that?

Aubrey Stiff, the Socialist reporter of the true-blue paper, was in more or less the same position as Colin Crisp on the other one, though he was a year younger and consequently less well adapted to the after-school world. He was eighteen, Colin nineteen. Colin had started as tea-boy in the city office. (When you speak of the City in East Anglia you do not mean that great black smudge on civilization, London, you mean Norwich, not yet a great black smudge.) Colin had landed in Radmere because his parents, on his father's retirement, had come to live on a new estate a mile from Radmere, where they were happy as fleas, his father making a new garden out of builders' rubble, his mother joining the WI, the Senior Club, the Flower Arrangers, you name anything suitable for a woman in her sixties of small brain and minimal education and she would join it. (This was her son's summing-up.) Well. OK for Pa and Ma and at least a jumping-off place for Colin; better than being a tea-boy in Norwich, though that first step had provided him with a name to present at the Radmere office. Colin was learning. Take any opening – you may not get another.

Aubrey was less happy in his work, which he had undertaken for Colin's reasons – any work was better than none, any pay would make him feel more like a man, less like his father's disappointment and his mother's baby. It was sad for him that his political faith, entered into simply as a rebellion against his parents, had no scope at all in his work. (Indeed, his ex-Army papa had got him the job with the true-blue paper.)

The two boys sometimes encountered one another when circling round on their bicycles looking for news in the off-time between weddings, boring non-fatal accidents, and funerals. They met, leaning on their bicycles, on Willington Green.

'Hello, any luck?'

'Not a sausage. This feud thing between the Brigadier and the shop-steward seems to have fizzled out.'

'One can see why. Money talks. They're bound over in a sum which isn't chicken-feed either for a retired Brigadier or a retired shop-steward. It must be hateful for both of them to realize that neither has the advantage of the other,' said Colin Crisp who didn't care, so had had some thought to spare on the rather pathetic facts of the issue.

Aubrey, who had opinions, said, 'The old boy *did* do the shooting, he hurt the dog, he fired at what's-his-name, and he'd been popping off at unsocial hours for ages. He ought to've got it in the neck. What's-his-name only *spoke* of setting fire to the house, in the heat of the moment, he didn't *do* anything. It's not really fair that they should both be treated alike. But it's what you'd expect of a Bench made up of local gentry. The old military man was on it himself, wasn't he, until he was retired under the age rule? Well, I ask you! They hang together, of course they do.'

'Lest they hang separately, at the hands of you lot,' grinned Colin.

'Right. How right you are,' said Aubrey. 'But it's all gone dead, for now. This school thing seems the only interest. You weren't at that Grammar, were you?'

'No. Norwich, bigger and better,' said Colin. 'Where were you?'

Aubrey hesitated, then came clean. 'A bloody expensive private prep-school where I learnt nothing except how not to cry when I was miserable or beaten, then a bloody expensive boarding school which was on the outer fringe of Public, where I learnt a lot of things my parents would have been horrified at and got three O-levels by the skin of my teeth.

I'm not really well up in this Grammar versus Comprehensive fight.'

'You ought to be, you with your politics,' said Colin, and explained the contretemps due to occur because of scrapping the exam without taking into account the snobbery of parents and the shortage of room at the Grammar. 'The exam wasn't good, but *this* is a shambles. Anyway it'll be worth watching. Hang round, the first few days of term, with your notebook hidden and your dark glasses on. See you.'

'Shall I recognize you, with *your* dark glasses on?'

'Better not, anyway. Hard enough to get information. I take it the boss-man's in with the County so won't admit it's a mess; I may be doing him wrong, but he's a well-paid employee of the County. The junior staff will be the ones who bear the brunt and feel the worst about it. Why should I tell you your job, laddie? You're my competitor.'

Aubrey, though younger and less experienced, gave Colin a straight look and said, 'Competitor my eye. We are both paid to bring in hard news. We aren't paid much but it's a springboard. See you in Fleet Street.'

'Gawd, I hope there's more hard news in Fleet Street. You going to the Foulger funeral tomorrow? Farmed in the county for umpteen years, never did anything else but beget three daughters; but a huge turn-out at the funeral, my God, how village people love funerals (more room for the living, is it?). And poor us, we have to get all the names, and all the spelling right, not only for the congregation but for the Floral Tributes. Hell, Aubrey, was this why I was born?'

'Was this why *I* was born?' echoed Aubrey.

'Don't be too cast down. It's something, to be able to collect a lot of boring facts and spell everything right. Most of our contemporaries, laddie, can't,' said Colin. 'I hope I wasn't born for nothing else but this, but time will show, and time will show for you too. See you in Fleet Street.'

They met again quite soon, sitting on a stone tomb in Radmere churchyard to eat the ham and cheese rolls they had respectively bought for lunch. They had a good view down the whole length of the market place and most of the chief though narrow shopping street which led down to a junction with the main east-west traffic stream. The narrow street was being dug up, as usual. For months it had been either dug up or obstructed by demolition and rebuilding. At first. motorists had tended to use other streets, to avoid the control-lights; this had greatly improved conditions for shoppers. But quite soon motorists went back to their old ways, which, in combination with the obstructions, made conditions far worse than they had ever been before.

'Ought to be a Pedestrian Precinct,' said Colin.

'What a mouthful. A Foot Street,' said Aubrey. Then on a kind of squeal, 'Hey, what's up?'

A small and growing cluster of people was below, where the market place narrowed into the shopping street.

Both boys abandoned their food and tumbled down the steps and raced down the market place, clawing their pockets for notebooks and pencils.

And when they got there, nothing much.

An old lady, on the pavement with her shopping basket had been bunted in the back by a lorry, also on the pavement because it could not otherwise have passed the obstruction. But instead of falling down and breaking something – even her nose would have been better than nothing – she pitched into the arms of a stalwart approaching male pedestrian, and no harm was done except to her temper, which was greatly inflamed. This, however, was not news. People's tempers had been inflamed almost continuously for about eighteen months. The lorry was off and away, and her rage was not against the driver, but against Them. *They* should

127

keep motors off so narrow a street, with its two-foot pavements, except at early and late hours for making deliveries to the shops. All this was stale stuff to the reporter-lads. It had been chewed over and over by the whole town, and the whole catchment area indeed.

They went back to their tomb, but some dog had found the remains of their lunch.

'Isn't it boring?' grumbled Aubrey. 'Nothing ever happens in the country. You think a happening is brewing up, then it all goes flat. Nobody shot anybody at Willington Green, the school thing's fizzled out, no strike, and room found somehow for everyone, and now an accident which wasn't. Just one vast non-event, that's country life.'

Colin, from his one-year advantage, said temperately, 'Possibly, life anywhere, don't you think? How many people do you personally know who have been murdered, raped, suicided, or killed or maimed on the roads? I don't know a single one. Not one. It must have been a bit different in the war, of course. We weren't born then. But it wasn't very different in the country. My grandparents just went on farming, and my father helped them, and did his Dad's Army bit in his spare time.'

'My grandparents were both killed in the Blitz,' said Aubrey, with the air of one scoring several points. 'Now *that* must have been a happening, the Blitz I mean. My father was in the war, retired as a major, but nothing as bad as that happened to him.'

'There are still odd bits of wars, pretty nasty, all over the world, if that's what you want,' said Colin. 'Bloody-minded little twerp, aren't you?'

'Well, it's all so deadly boring – '

'If you ask me, more history is made out of the deadly boring, by those who endure it, than by big loud bangs,' said Colin.

'But what are *we* supposed to fill our notebooks with?'

'I've a wedding out at Pye this afternoon. Haven't you?'

'God, yes. But people get married and buried all the time. It's all repetition, except for trying to spell the names right.'

'Don't you eat breakfast every morning, snatch a bite for lunch, etc. etc. until bed-time? Threescore years and ten, maybe more, of repetition. It's all repetition. That's life. We've got the Late Summer Flower Show on Saturday – '

'Oh, hell. Lists of names, people *and* flowers, to spell right, hundreds of them – '

'And the same again next year and the year after. And not only the Late Summer show: the Spring, the Summer and the Autumn. The seasons repeat themselves. Everything does. Winter's a sort of refuge from Flower Shows, but people still get born and married and buried, even in winter. It's all getting the names roight, bor, you dew that and you dew yar job.'

'It stinks.'

'It teaches you accuracy, kid, and maybe something else, a polite approach to people so that they'll actually *tell* you how to spell their names. Perhaps you don't need politeness – you've been better brought-up than me – but I had to learn to put on a smile and ask nicely. Didn't come natural at all, but what was I to do with a name like Bassingthwaighte, with half a dozen superfluous letters in it, or come to that Featherstonehaugh pronounced peanuts? Politeness and accuracy are useful lessons.'

'Thank you, kind sir, for your words of wisdom,' said Aubrey with an elaborate sneer, the best way to avoid admitting that neither his upbringing nor his expensive schooling had prepared him for those two names.

After a pause he asked, 'Feather-stone-haw pronounced *what*?'

'Fan-shaw, that's what I first wrote down. But some

occult Power guided me and I asked, with a nice deferential smile, and I got it from the horse's mouth. That's triumph. (When I was at Grammar I got a rocket from the old tartar who taught English for spelling that word trumph-ump. I still think it's good. I was so keen to write, I couldn't wait to spell.)'

'And this tedious job's taught you?'

'Not to spell, but to find out how. To ask and get replies, kind ones, friendly ones. If or when we get to Fleet Street, you know, people we interview have got to like us, or we'll get nothing. No good shouting at them, or coming the gentleman, that's you, young Aubrey, *they're* the givers, *we're* the askers. We learn the rudiments of the technique here, on our local weekly rags.'

'With your gift of the gab you ought to run for Parliament,' said Aubrey, trying to be even more sneerful than he was before, because he knew that Colin was right, totally right as far as this limited job of theirs was concerned. A bloody boring ill-paid job – but it had its uses. It was a step. Aubrey wondered if it was a step in the right direction; Colin didn't – he had ink in his veins. Colin was headed in the right direction. Aubrey had his doubts. Neither of them had any parental guidance or approval. In Colin's case, parental regret, in Aubrey's, parental disapproval. Why did a farmer's boy want to go into journalism, and why the hell didn't a soldier's boy want to go into the Army? It had not been said, and perhaps it never would be, 'Because I hate my father.'

The fathers did not know.

But the hatred of boys for their fathers goes on and on. If it did not, the world would stick in its rut.

12
Things That Don't Get Into The Papers

Quite suddenly, Jimmy was carted off to the geriatric ward of the local hospital. Janey felt awful about it, but she could not have helped fainting in sheer exhaustion while hauling a load of heavy wet bedclothes off Jimmy's bed. A big man, he liked a big bed; bedmaking had been a heavy task for Janey for some years – and now *wet* beds . . . Well, the good kind daily would do the washing . . .

The good kind daily heard a peculiar thump on the floor above her head, and trotted up to investigate. What was Mr Jim up to? She felt responsible for the two poor old dears for whom she worked.

In Jimmy's large bedroom there was Jimmy in his dressing-gown, sitting smiling – when was he not smiling? – by the window, and, goodness, Miss Janey on the floor half smothered in blankets and sheets. Raised in the arm of her helper, Janey came round and said, 'Oh, how silly of me, I'm so sorry.'

No good asking Jimmy where the brandy, if any, was. This latest turn of his (no mistaking the smell of wet bed) meant complete regression. He was a child again. Perhaps he always had been.

The good kind daily rang the doctor, the doctor came and called the ambulance. Janey was weeping, but as much with relief as with any sense of guilt or sorrow. The doctor, who knew all about the case, knew she had nothing to feel guilty about, and very little to feel sorry about, since Jimmy didn't know Monday from Tuesday. Feed him and keep him warm, he'd be all right.

'But there are his plants, Davy,' sobbed Janey to the doctor. 'His last hold on life, his greenhouse plants. He went on knowing about *them* when he'd forgotten everything else.'

'Then you take a plant every time you visit him. The nurses will water them. God knows where we find the good girls, the good women, but we do. He'll be happy, more than most because he has a happy disposition to start with. And *you* can have a rest from work and worry.'

'How long will they keep him in hospital?' Janey was already worrying about the thick, heavy, interior-spring mattress – how could it be cleaned, did the Cleaners take such things, how to dispose of it if they didn't?

'Depends,' said the doctor. 'Long enough for you to have a good rest, because what's to happen if you collapse?'

'Goodness, yes, I *can't* collapse,' she agreed. And lay blissfully in bed until afternoon, when she consumed a bowl of Bovril with bread in it and prepared to visit Jimmy in the geriatric ward.

He was lightly sedated but he knew her, and impressed upon her the importance of watering the greenhouse plants. He had no complaints on his own account, his big smiling face was as trouble-free as ever: but he laid it on heavily about watering the plants. And she promised to bring him the large crimson gloxinia just coming into bloom. 'Nurse will look after it, won't you, dear, and stand it where he can see it?'

Young Nurse Alger smiled and said yes while her heart bled for both of them. Jimmy's days were numbered and Janey's did not look too bright. Her thin cheeks were very highly coloured and she must surely be at least a stone underweight. The wagtail and the cuckoo.

Young Nurse Alger supposed Janey to be Jimmy's wife, and she was not far wrong. No wife could have loved and cared for Jimmy better than his widowed sister. But there was a shock for Janey when, in October, after a week in coma, Jimmy faded out.

The house, the impressive house, the big house of the village, too big, of course, for Janey alone, but of considerable value, was left in Jimmy's Will to a Mrs Gathercole of somewhere in the Midlands, a woman of whom Janey had never heard – but alas, she did exist: Jimmy's lawyers hunted her out. What she had been to Jimmy or Jimmy to her, Janey had no means of discovering. What she did know was that she herself was left without a roof over her head or any capital with which to buy one. She had her Old Age Pension about which she was shamefaced because she did not think it was meant for the sisters of Company Chairmen, and a minuscule First World War pension for the husband whom she had almost forgotten. Could she afford Deanery House? Could she endure Deanery House? No and no. She had a car and a driving licence, she was not a helpless old thing needing to be waited on or to hire some other person to drive her. But where could she live? You can't live in a car. It would be fun but it wasn't allowed.

The bush telegraph got busy as soon as strangers were seen entering Fen Lodge, a man and woman in their fifties, a younger man who might be their son, and another middle-aged who was patently a lawyer because of his brief-case, and was personally known to at least one observer. This unfamiliar quartet, their faces subsequently seen at windows upstairs and down, departed after a time. Mrs Peters had not been seen at all. The kind daily, Mrs Self, simply said she was 'out'.

Well, Janey was selling the house; this was the first thought. And very sensible – it had been too big for two, so it was far too big for one. But Mrs Self knew better. She had been not only a daily but a friend, for many years. Janey had told her.

So it was not long before Harriet Brandling heard the naked truth: a legacy of five hundred pounds for Janey (might as well be five hundred pence, these days, said Harriet) and nothing else. Nothing.

Who were those other people? It hardly mattered. The Will was in their favour and they existed. The middle-aged man was most likely an illegit. of Jimmy's; big handsome smiling Jimmy could have had a score of women, fifty years before. And here was a son, also a grandson. How old was the Will? It couldn't matter. Fifty years, thirty years, twenty years. It had not taken much account of Janey Peters, who had made Fen Lodge such a comfortable home for Jimmy's later life. But it was authentic, and the beneficiaries were alive and kicking. And for Janey Peters, five hundred pounds flat.

Harriet did not even ask Harold, who might not remember who Janey Peters was. She rang up Janey and said, 'Come and stay with us for a bit while you get your bearings. It isn't Buckingham Palace but it's restful, and we have loads of room, for weeks or months if you fancy it. Do give it a thought.'

'But – '

'But you and I are on the same wave-length.'

'We *can't* be: you're a famous writer – '

'Careful with your adjectives, gal. I am a well-known writer. But does that set me apart from the human race? A thousand times no, I'm just one of the humans who can use words. Some use music, some use pencils and paints. Some are cooks, some are nurses, some are farmers, some – too many – fancy themselves as scientists, and far too many go adventuring into stocks and shares, bits of paper which may be worthless tomorrow. You and I will get on all right. Do come. You need a bit of peace and quiet.'

So Janey packed the few things which really belonged to her, and drove along the very minor road to Colham Hall, escaping death at least three times because she was a good driver with quick reactions, who could climb a bank or pop sideways into a gateway when confronted by a cattle-lorry taking up three-fifths of the road.

'You've a little second-floor flat, love, if you want to be alone, but not if you don't,' said Harriet. Like all north-country people she found the word 'love' come readily to her tongue. Whether these dismal East Anglians understood the easy friendliness of love, or confined it to passion, or knew nothing about it at all, did not worry Harriet. She had grown up with a wide-spreading cheerful love and it remained with her. Harold had never wanted love except the bed variety, which was so difficult to fake up when all the other varieties were missing.

Harold would probably dislike having Janey as a semi-permanent guest, but Harriet had long ceased to care about

135

Harold's likes and dislikes. Janey needed a roof over her head and a bit of affection and she was going to get them, for as long as she needed them.

So there was one thing settled, temporarily at least, in the catchment area that September. But there was another conflict still unresolved. Neither of these was Press material, nor widely known except among friends, and the Carlyons, newcomers to the area, had no local friends anyway.

They, a couple with two children, had moved into a Victorian terraced-house on the main through-road which raced along the ugly part of Radmere on the way to or from the Midlands and the coast. The terrace, tall and of grey brick (perhaps once yellow) was unattractive on the outside despite little balustraded flights of steps from the pavement to each front door, and quite appalling on the inside, the houses high and thin, and with dark basements for the servants, believe it or not. No gardens in front, only the steps to the pavement, and very narrow strips of garden behind because the houses themselves were so narrow. These manifold disadvantages had reduced the cost of the house to the Carlyons, Empire-building class but on the beach through lack of Empire.

The daughter, nineteen, was a disappointment to her father but a source of satisfaction to her mother. She had gone her own way and to hell with Empire: she had trained, on grants, as a teacher, and was working in a Primary School a few miles off. This was one of the reasons, but not the chief, for regarding Radmere as a possible home for the family. The other child, a son, was ten years younger, owing to the absence of Dad in an unhealthy part of Empire. This boy Charles was at an expensive prep-school on the East Coast, and this was another and stronger reason for finding a cheap house at Radmere, only thirty miles away. Charles hated every minute of school; Dad hated paying for it, but had

his *class* to think of, his own education having been paid
for by his parents, though he managed not to mention his
very obscure Prep and Public Schools. Education, however
bad, if paid for meant class.

The move to Radmere, and the boy's school-fees for last
term, had left the Carlyons skint. So Alice tried once more:

'Hubert, the Grammar School here has a good reputation.
Charles couldn't do worse than he's doing at his Prep.'

Hubert knew how to deal with Alice. He bawled, 'Make a
man of him, get him away from Mummy's skirts.'

'But he isn't learning anything, his reports are awful. He
might be a lunatic, by what they say. Do you want a lunatic,
Hubert?'

The one good thing which had come to Hubert from his
undistinguished educational career was that a man did not
clobber a woman of his own class. He did not now hit his
wife, he never had, he merely yelled at her, 'You stupid bitch,
what do you know about it?'

'I was educated better than you,' said Alice.

'At a filthy stinking High School.'

'Where I was taught to write and spell, and I might have
been trained for something but for the war. What about
you?'

'*I* managed *men*.'

'I suppose any man with a loud enough yell can frighten
other men into obedience. But could you write down an
account of your doings, Hubert?'

'Write down? I had a babu in an office to do that kind of
thing. If Charlie doesn't learn how to manage men, he'll
end up like my clerk, writing things down, poor devil. No
action, no power. Just writing things down. And your
bloody Grammar School does not give a boy the standing to
do anything else. What do Grammar Schools produce?
Teachers for other Grammar Schools. Not *men*.'

Alice looked at her red, hairy, middle-aged, stupid Man and loathed him.

But what could she do? Having been shouted at for weeks on end she had relinquished the bit of money she had had from her father, in part-payment for the horrible tall thin house on the Radmere through-road, where the traffic ceased not to roar day or night. There was sleep to be had in the back bedrooms if one took a pill.

And this was a little old market-town, beautiful in the parts north of the through-road. But as bad as London where the Carlyons had acquired their tall thin house.

About fifty yards away there was a Caff or Cayfe, open day and night, where roaring vehicles shrieked to a halt and after an interval their drivers battered each other, out in the road, until the police arrived. That was Alice's impression, though the rowdies might well have been motor-bikers or mere j.ds.

'This is life in a dear little country town,' said Alice, but Hubert did not know what she meant because he had been on very strong sleeping-pills for years. He could have slept through an air-raid, indeed he had. In the morning he was heavy, glum and stupid, but Alice knew how glad she ought to be to have him knocked out at night: no sex, no fears about conception. He was a human log, who required her to feed him and keep him clean because that was what she had promised to do, in the presence of witnesses, in a church more than twenty years ago.

She was not minded to renege on her bargain (since it was about as bad for Hubert as for her) provided young Charles could be saved from insanity. She thought he might be if he lived at home and 'went to Grammar' – which he could now, however backward, on parents' say-so. He would not have to spend twelve weeks howling, either in class or in the san. He was scared stiff, poor kid, because his prospects of Public School, either on brains or on brawn, were very feeble, and what would Dadda say? The wretched child had cried most of his little life for fear of Dadda, but he suffered even more at boarding school than at home, because there were other awful people at school, but there was Mother at home. This was well understood by Alice.

But she had no leverage, she had no money, she had given her small nest-egg to Hubert for that hideous tall thin terrace house because it was fairly near to both her children. If Hubert could raise the school-fees for the prep-school by one of his tortuous insurance practices (which engaged him in a lifelong game of robbing Peter to pay Paul) Charlie would go back to prep-school and cry solidly for another term; and Alice could not contemplate leaving Hubert – taking Charlie with her of course – because she had no money nor any qualifications for earning money. Charlie was Hubert's puppet, and Hubert was bent on shoving Charlie into the class he himself had barely attained, and rising higher through Charlie if he could.

'Oh, God,' muttered Alice, granddaughter of a deceased Bart., 'what's all this about class as long as the people in it do proper work and like it? Phyl does.'

'Phyl teaches the rudiments to the Great Unwashed,' said Hubert.

'And why not? She's good at it, and somebody must.'

'Why? The polloi were better off not knowing anything but labour,' said he.

'And where do you draw the line between you and them?' said Alice, a pulse beating in her throat. 'You might say I'm a step above you, but since I married you I've been your household slut, I empty your jerry and wash your stinking underpants, while you never turn your hand to anything but golf and you're no genius at *that* either. If that's being a gentleman you can stuff it,' said Alice.

For the first time in his life he roared like a bull and raised his hand to her; but she, small and nippy, ducked and butted him in the stomach. Not hard enough. But hard enough to surprise him.

'The Upper Class at play,' she said, before leaving and carefully shutting the door behind her. She only needed a thirty-second start, to get out of range of an adversary so much slower and heavier.

And so she discovered the unsuspected advantage of having the public street just outside the front door. On the pavement was safety; there was so much traffic in the street both on foot and on wheels. It was nice to know that this beastly house had an escape-hatch.

She was not altogether displeased that Hubert had at last 'raised his hand to her'. It put him in his place. She would not let him forget that he was no gentleman.

A third reason for choosing the beastly house was that it was near the railway station (good fast service to London and Norwich) and the bus-park (so-so service to neighbouring towns). And when neither would do, as in conveying Charlie to school, it was cheaper to hire a car than to keep a car of one's own. The school-fees had occasioned this choice: private prep-school *or* car. So the Carlyons had no car.

Alice regretted this. Her rattly old second-hand bicycle had so limited a range. She never wanted to go to London or Norwich or the larger local towns: Hubert was the one who attended Old Boys' reunions and shopped expensively for clothes, shoes and golf-clubs: Alice found the Radmere shops more than adequate for country requirements, and Charlie's school uniform came by post from Harrods. But she would have enjoyed seeing more of the new countryside than the old bike allowed: it would not go fast enough to get her home in time to cook Hubert's meals. People told her of half a score of huge cathedral-like parish churches within, say, ten miles, some of them standing alone amid fields (why?), besides several old windmills, mostly farther away, restored to working order by enthusiasts. Hubert said she had a bits-and-pieces mind: well, these were her bits and pieces. Someone, not Hubert, might have thought of a better name for her interests, such as Rural Social History. But whatever the name, she could not do much to further these interests because she was Hubert's servant. He had married her to obtain a cook-general, and she had married him to be kept. That was how it went. Nearly a generation earlier, that was how it went for Irene Gault too (but the Gaults and the Carlyons were as yet unacquainted).

The hired car came for Charlie. He had been sick twice before breakfast, and had eaten no breakfast.

'I'd better go with him,' said Alice. 'One of us must, for the sake of appearances, and you won't want him catting all over your best suit.'

Hubert revealed the depths of his cowardice by agreeing to this. He wanted the credit without the suffering. So Charlie, aged ten and very small and thin, slept against his mother's shoulder for most of the trip. When he was awakened by the pull-up of the car at the door of the one-time mansion, now human factory, he started howling. He recognized the place instantly. Alice grabbed him and hauled him up the impressive steps, demanded of the major-domo to see the Headmaster, and without waiting for an answer dragged Charlie along the well-known path to the Study. And barged in.

'Hello, Doctor Stewkley, here we are, and *what* a good advertisement for your educational establishment!'

Another family, Pa, Ma and frightened little son aged perhaps eight, were already in the Study. Alice had a natural upper-class accent, Alice's child was in a natural convulsion of sobs, the other family, new to the job, gaped and trembled.

141

'Ah, little Carlyon,' exclaimed the Head, grinning like a gargoyle.

'Just about right for the abattoir,' said Alice. 'Young and tender. Shall I take him to Matron?'

'Oh, yes, please,' babbled the Head, completely off balance, only aware that she must be making a terribly bad impression on the new set of parents.

'You'll let me have the skin and bones back, won't you?' came Alice's light, cultivated, sweet but highly audible voice as she pushed the sobbing Charlie before her and departed.

Dr Stewkley said, 'I think she finds it hard to confess that her little boy is far from manly and that *she* has spoilt him: so she puts a satirical face on it; a kind of courage, I suppose.' This, he thought, would keep him at his proper lofty level. 'But your boy, I am sure, is neither cowardly nor spoilt.'

At precisely the same moment, Matron, a big woman with a kind patient horse-face, was saying to Alice, 'Oh, dear, I did hope you would realize that Charlie is either too young or too tender for this set-up. He'll have to go straight into the san; he's running a temperature.' She knew this simply by putting her experienced palm against his forehead.

'It's not me, it's his father, Matron dear,' said Alice. 'Is there a way you could keep in touch, with neither the Head nor my husband knowing?'

'We'll think of something. Boarding schools for little kids are sickening,' said Matron, 'but at least we don't have some untrained girl with a crush on the games-master calling herself a Matron. I will look after your poor little fish. Is there a time of day when your husband is always out, so that I could telephone you?'

'There's no time when he's always out because he doesn't do any work,' said Alice, 'and besides, we're not on the telephone. We can't afford it. It's the school-fees.'

'Don't think you are alone in this, Mrs Carlyon,' said

Matron grimly. 'Education-snobbery is pauperizing the Middle Class, and for all I know the Upper Class as well, though we don't get any of them here. Give me the number of your nearest telephone-box and make sure you are there every day at a certain time, a time when you could reasonably be out shopping or something. If there is no ring within five minutes, push off: the situation will be in hand. But every day, Mrs Carlyon, at least for the first week. I'll tell you if you can ease off.'

'Oh, Matron, you're clever. *You've done this before,*' said Alice, big-eyed.

'Yes, I'm sorry to say I've had to do it before. I cannot make the Stewkleys realize that not all little boys are made of snips and snails and puppy dogs' tails. They never had any little boys, only Afghan Hounds. Nice elegant things but not quite like small frightened kids torn from their mothers' arms.'

'To be turned into imitation he-men, stupid, murderous, as soon as possible. My little boy isn't one of those, he'll never be made into a he-man like his father I hope: just into a happy man with a few thoughts in his head. But he won't even *live* if he's terrified into running a fever all the time.'

'I know, Mrs Carlyon, I know. I'll do all I can.'

13
Medical

Little Carlyon came home by ambulance, after a fortnight
in the san, feverish, weeping and unable to eat. Matron had
kept Alice informed, and at last the Head had written to
Hubert, declining further responsibility for so puny a specimen
of humanity. 'Our doctor,' wrote the Head, meaning not,
of course, a doctor attached to the school, but the local
GP, 'can find nothing organically wrong with the lad. I
conclude that the trouble is mental, and should be dealt
with at some sort of special school; Charles has certainly
seemed unable to learn anything, in the two years he has
been with us.'

Hubert, while the ambulance was still on its way, received
this letter and went straight up the wall, yelling at Alice
from the height he thought he had attained, 'See what you've
done, with your infernal Mummying, made an idiot of my
son!'

'Well, I hope you'll make less noise when he arrives,' said Alice. 'He's a very sick little boy, and I suppose you don't want a *dead* son. Unless you keep your voice down, I'll get into the ambulance with him and go on to the Jenny Lind Hospital.'

'Fuss, fuss, fuss! Women!' shouted Hubert.

'I suppose you never had a mother, you were born of spontaneous combustion, you give that impression,' said Alice.

'Of course I had a mother but I was sent away to school before I was eight,' said Hubert, 'and no nonsense.'

'And see what it did for *you*,' Alice finished in her icicle-tinkling tones. 'It's not yet a crime to send a small child, male or female, away from home to strangers and a strange discipline. But one day, live long enough, it'll be a crime.'

'You do talk bloody rot. How's a boy to become a man unless he gets away from petticoats?'

'At eight years old or even less? That's the crime,' said Alice. 'How did you enjoy your first few terms at a boarding school? No good asking because you won't tell the truth. You've been a stunning success all your life, in your own eyes. But you didn't get into a proper Public School, did you? You've scraped along, and here we are, in this ghastly house on a noisy road and with no money and no car. You're *not* an authority on how to bring up little boys, Hubert. Either you were bashed into submission at eight years old, or you were too thick-headed to be bashed. Either way, you didn't take in much education.'

'Have you quite finished? I learnt to manage *men*.'

'By yelling and whip-cracking. Like the slave-drivers of a hundred years before. Any thick-skulled Simon Legree can do that.'

'They weren't slaves – '

'No, they earned small wages. They could quit if they were brave enough. But you howled and shouted and yelled at them till they thought they were beset by devils. They were simple, quiet, gentle darkies – '

'Mau-mau were simple gentle quiet, you bloody idiot?'

'Yes, until they had to take more than they could bear,' said Alice. 'They were men, like you, they had a sort of inborn pride, however stupid, like you.'

'Not like me. I'm not a Black,' shouted Hubert.

'Pity, in a way,' said Alice. 'That silly dirty red skin, you couldn't call it white, has given you an unjustified conceit of yourself. A man's a man for a' that, you know. No difference, the same set of problems, only a variable scale of incomes.'

'You bloody bitch!' trumpeted Hubert. This was his usual last word. And he was lucky. The ambulance drew up at the kerb at that moment.

Matron was in it. She said to Alice, 'I couldn't let him be alone with strangers. Can you get me back to the school?'

'We don't have a car. The school-fees, you know. And there's no railway in that direction and we'd have to find out about buses.'

'I'll hire a taxi.'

'My husband can ruddy well hire a taxi.'

And Hubert was so shocked by the sight of his tiny thin son, white as paper and shut-eyed, that he telephoned the taxi company without demur. He had not seen. Seeing is important. He had not seen that the son of his loins could be other than a stupid little toughie like his father. He had not seen. But now he saw a dying child. And his child, not a doubt of it, his only male child. Dying.

And he did not feel like ranting or yelling: he was scared to the marrow, and only too ready to leave to Alice the whole business of nursing, at which he knew he would be quite useless. His essential cowardice came to the surface. Alice made him go up the town and do the household shopping, go to the launderette with the washing, and he did. Anything rather than sit by the bedside of the dying child.

Who decided, after two days of peace and no further view of his father than that awful purple face glaring into the ambulance, not to die. Or his body decided for him, nourished by Alice on good soup and a nice-tasting sparkling drink. She too consumed the soup and the drink, sitting beside his bed, and this was an encouragement.

'Mummy, do I have to go back to school?'

'Not that school. Not away from home.'

The appetite definitely perked up after this. But Alice did not hasten Charlie's return to life. The more Hubert suffered, the better. Charlie was playing draughts and dominoes long before Hubert knew that a small coffin would not be needed.

'I do have to go to school somewhere, Mummy.'

'Well, there are several. The first one is the Middle School, seven to eleven. After that, we'll see whether the Grammar or the Mod. will suit you.'

'*And I can live here?*'

'Yes, except for school dinner. The Middle School is just across the road and up that footpath.'

'I know. I wanted to go there.'

'You never said so, not even to me.'

'What was the use? You can't do anything against Dadda, and Dadda wouldn't have taken a blind bit of notice, he'd just have shouted at you and me both,' said the ten-year-old.

'He won't shout now; we've the doc behind us,' said Alice. Their new local GP had been called in, had found that Charlie, with his matchstick legs and arms, weighed as much as a normal five-year-old, and had discovered the cause of this malnutrition: terror, and not only at school. 'He hardly eats anything in the holidays either,' said Alice, 'not at meals. If nobody's looking, he'll be tempted by some fancy stuff like ice-cream.'

'Very good, ice-cream,' said the doc. 'Keep him upstairs, except for running about a bit in the garden, as long as you can, so he won't feel his eating is being watched and criticized and won't be scared by any – er – '

'Eruptions,' said Alice.

'Exactly; sudden outbreaks of noise, from whatever cause. And feed him ice-cream or anything else he likes, between meals. If he makes up his weight he might be fit for school again after Christmas. But not to go *away*, defenceless you know: it doesn't suit every child. It suited me, probably it suited your husband, that's why he was so set on it. But we are slowly learning that we are not all cast in the same mould.'

This doc was a youngish man, the junior partner in the outfit. The Carlyons, newcomers, naturally had to take the younger, newer man. The older doctor's 'list' was full of friends, who paid, and longstanding panel-patients from 'way back'. The new younger doctor would not get any who paid . . . unless Hubert Carlyon thought it was beneath his 'class' to accept free medicine even though he was taxed for it. This notion had never entered the young doc's head. He existed to relieve suffering, and, if he could, save life. And he was paid for it (not on a madly generous scale, but enough) so he could give his whole attention to the job. Whether that oaf Hubert Carlyon, whom he had met a couple of times on the golf-course, paid or did not pay was of no moment to him; though he was engaged, his girl was no scrounger, she was already laying plans for a career of her own in teaching or social service, for when the two children they hoped for were old enough to be semi-detached from her. The world in which young Doctor Smythe and his Anthea lived was not the world in which old Doctor Cooper and Mrs Cooper lived. The sad thing was that the Coopers had grown-up married children who seemed not to know that the world had changed. An awful lot of misunderstanding lay at the door of parents. They did their best but they were mostly behind the times. Lucky for poor little Charlie Carlyon that his mother was up-to-date: his pa clearly wasn't. But Charlie, if he lived, could enter the modern world.

Would he live, poor little tadpole? Only if his mother was able to circumvent his father, that was plain.

The father and the mother belonged to different generations, or possibly to systems of education with different outlooks. Either way, Carlyon and his wife were at odds, and this was not a good prospect for the poor little terrified son. Yelled at, no doubt, long before he knew what he had done wrong. Because, quite possibly, Dad felt at a disadvantage *vis-à-vis* Mum. Class! In the world of young Doctor Smythe, a bloody bit of nonsense. But he knew well enough that it did not look like nonsense to his parents' generation. Or to his elderly partner's generation.

So stupid, to try to make a *social* dividing-line. Young Doctor Smythe had been at school with the sons and grandsons of noblemen: some of the boys could be taught nothing, not elementary grammar, spelling or arithmetic; and were not even very good at their hereditary sports of cricket and shooting. A few were normal bright lads, game for anything. Where then was the dividing-line? Would you include the idiots in the Upper Class – and if so, for God's sake *why*? Oafs, or was it oaves, the lot of them. The bright ones among the courtesy-titles were fit to take their place as high-up as they could find a place, and so were the Tom Smythes and the sons of many and many a market-gardener, railway-porter, fisherman and even perhaps thief. Brains, not ancestry were the requirement – they were not mutually exclusive though it often seemed so.

Hubert Carlyon had no brains. Alice Carlyon had quite a lot though not much chance to make an independence out of them because of her unlucky marriage. Little Charlie, the 'patient' was too young for predictions. His brains, if any, had been scared out of his head by his stupid yelling father and that class-oriented school. Hubert Carlyon had not much class so his son had been sent home. Had Hubert been the Hon. or Sir, the school would not have parted so readily: Charlie Carlyon might have been condemned to death.

'I've got him now,' said the young doc to himself, 'and I'll save him if I can.'

He said this at greater length, adding, 'I don't care if he's a genius or an ordinary little bloke, he's entitled to his chance,' to his girl Anthea, who sometimes came to see him in his alien and backward environment.

She said, 'How right you are. They come in all sorts, even the ones with funny-peculiar parents like this kid – '

'The mum isn't funny-peculiar. Just trying to be sensible against heavy odds. There's a nearly grown-up daughter training to be a real person, Pa disgruntled about it. It doesn't get called a Broken Home, Anthy, because the parents are still together, but it's as badly broken a home as any I've yet had to deal with.'

'Homes can be in fragments, while still under the same roof,' agreed Anthea. 'Mine was. They didn't divorce until I was of age and able to earn a living. I can't tell you how I longed to be free of them, years before, never mind earning a living, just to be free of the bickering and shouting. I was disgusted. I didn't want to grow up into that sort of person. But they thought they were doing right for me, by living in the same house until I got a not-too-bad job.'

'Oh, Anthy, if I'd had enough money to marry you

sooner – '

'Darling, don't worry. It was all experience. I don't think people, male or female, ought to marry straight out of the schoolroom, do you?'

'Oh, Anthy, my dear sweet, you are such a sensible girl!'

'Keep me posted about that poor little kid.'

'If he lives, yes.' And the young doc watched his Anthea disappear from his sight in the fast diesel train which was one of Radmere's sources of pride.

The medical arrangements in the catchment area were perhaps less muddled and less in crisis than some of the other public services such as Education and the District Councils. Not only Radmere and the other small towns in the area, Harbury, Bilgay, Bruckles, had their own set of doctors in partnership or in competition, but the larger villages on the fringes of the area were looked after by their own doctors too. Or perhaps 'Looked after', was not quite right: it was more 'Looked at'. One look, and off to hospital for tests or checks or whatever the GP had not the time for and possibly, these days, not the knowledge. Radmere was lucky. Young Doc Smythe, and a contemporary of his in the competing group, had been caught between wind and water, neither too old to be with-it nor so young as to be utterly without it. They believed in trying to treat their patients. Not that they could prescribe what the patients wanted, a tonic. There was no such thing any more as a tonic. There were vitamins, analgesics, words which meant nothing to the patients, so it was no wonder that the patients went to chemists, not doctors, for the tonics which had kept their parents and grand-parents alive to a respectable old age. It seemed to the patients that doctors were pushing their responsibility on to hospitals, and that if the patient was daft enough to go to hospital he'd be cut open, if only that the top surgeon might show the houseman how to do it. The modern attitude to the medical profession was 'Keep away if you possibly can'. But this did not apply to youngish Doc Smythe or his contemporary in the other lot. The patients felt they were interested, well-informed and caring. And so did the patients in some of the fringe-village groups. A doctor wouldn't even settle down to work there, unless he cared for his patients. There was no fortune to be made, there was just a valuable job to be done. Without, except in extremis, surgeons' knives.

Keeping people on an even keel; keeping them able to do their work, so that they did not have to fear cutting-down to the level of the dole, or if they were too long unfit, an even lower level. A lot of the doctor's work was to cheer and comfort men – chiefly men – who had never been ill in their lives and on the first onset of something not necessarily fatal were convinced that their wives would be widowed and their children fatherless in less than no time. Comfort, that was the doc's first objective; because after comfort, the patient often rallied, and between them doctor and patient often achieved a cure.

This, however, was not understood by the new boys in the profession, who had to drag Science in, and Science was very uncomforting to the countryman. Electrocardiograph – wires in all directions and suckers plunked on his chest – scared him stiff. His heart behaved in a far from natural way when terrified. And in many other ways the shoving of the patient off to hospital instead of prescribing at home a tonic or a sedative or an aid to digestion produced symptoms which the unlucky patient had never had before – the symptoms of fear of death. Why would he be sent to hospital unless he had cancer or something worse if there *was* anything worse? It was possible to indicate to patients of a certain level of education that hospital tests were more thorough and accurate than anything the doctor could do at home: but it was not possible to indicate this to the farm-worker, the gardener, the general labourer. From years back, hospital to him meant death – that was what hospitals were for. And no young doc had the time, the patience or the knowledge of human nature to explain to the more humble of his patients the workings of the magic machines, all wires and lights and tick-tick noises, which would or indeed would not reveal what the patient had wrong with him. Science had added a great deal of mental suffering to the human race while explaining very little because it could not. There was such a great gulf between the suffering man and the scientist.

Who might be suffering too but would never admit it.

That was the crux. The man with the educated brains would confess to no weakness whatsoever, he was the Great I Am. What he said *went*. And he might be mad as a hatter, driven off course by his own fantasies. But no one could tell him, no one could stop him, because all self-styled scientists these days were a bit mad, and yet were respected and feared by all the non-scientists, who had neither enough confidence nor enough knowledge to cut them down to size. If a scientist said there was going to be an imminent collision between the planet Earth and some other heavenly body, who was qualified to tell him he was wrong? – Until, of course, his deadline was past and nothing had occurred. By then he had thought up a scientific excuse. Anyone with a degree in any branch of Science, physics, medicine, what-have-you, could readily bamboozle an entire population. Partly because the ignorant but ambitious wanted to climb on to the band-waggon, partly because the pig-ignorant took in, open-mouthed, what they were told by any person with letters after his or her name. How did he or she get the letters after the name, except for sheer ultimate *knowledge*? Some of the honest graduates might have said 'Because we're learning'. But the honest ones were few: the others said

'Because we know!'

But nobody knows anything except from long years of often painful living: the kind of experience which is *scientifically* known as trial-and-error. The common man's life is trial and error from birth to death. And if he's happy and can make a living he deserves a B or even DSc, because it's more than most of those fancy lads have managed.

Young Doc Smythe was one of the very rare birds in contemporary medicine: he believed there were some things he could manage on his own, at all events until the symptoms indicated otherwise, rather than scare the old, the simple and the little kids into fits by shipping them off to the strange and unexplained world of hospital, full of machinery, and top-surgeons who did not speak to patients, and sweet kind darkie nurses who had no information, only gentleness. To a very old person or a little child, even the gentlest of darkie nurses was a frightening alien. So sad, this nonsense about skin. But it existed. The Middle Class and the twenty-fives to sixties in age knew what they owed to immigrant nurses, but the little kids, the very old and the simpletons were not able to learn anything. So they were scared of black skins.

It might be better in large urban areas where there were lots of black-skinned men and women who had proved themselves to be just as good at their jobs as white-skinned men and women. But East Anglia was the last stronghold of the English, God help them.

Doc Smythe's elderly partner was always warning him against taking too much on himself, and was full of information about the various services available at the two general hospitals and the mental and geriatric establishments in the catchment area. He was rather obviously afraid that young Doc Smythe would make a boo-boo and give the Practice a bad name, and that would be a great pity, because the lad was easy to work with, never minded taking the night calls –

and there weren't all that many properly qualified boys wanting to be juniors in general practice, these days, when specialization paid so very much better in the long run.

'I assure you I can manage the Carlyon kid without sending him to hospital,' said young Doc Smythe to his senior. 'That would be a sentence of death, very possibly. Of course it would be easier if I could shoot the father, but you wouldn't let me do that, would you?'

It took Dr Cooper quite two seconds to realize that his junior partner was making a joke.

'Ah, one of those, is it? What's the mother like?'

'By no means a softie. But the dad's a volcano, so bad for a nervous undersized little kid. There will never come a time when that kid is big enough to clobber his dad – '

'Well, I hope not, I'm a dad myself,' said Dr Cooper.

'And your three are grown up, or nearly, and doing OK,' said young Doc Smythe. 'I just wonder if you had to throw your weight about a lot, and shout and threaten, to make them toe the line? I guess not, I guess you had too much sense, sir.'

Doc Cooper liked being called Sir. 'I confess it wasn't all smooth, particularly with Rosie, but I don't think I was a volcano. I don't think eruptions have a lasting effect. You must have noticed, Smythe, that after eruptions and even earthquakes, the people rebuild in exactly the same places. It seems quite idiotic, but it's what they want. So the eruption or the earthquake might as well not have happened. It's the same with explosive people. They become boring and ineffectual. Their families learn not to care. It's just poor old Pa sounding off again.'

'Poor little Carlyon is still at the stage of being scared by the noise.'

'Feed him vitamins and stuff, get some weight on him, he'll survive, and his father will be no more unnerving than a jet plane or a revving lorry. We live in a world befouled by noise – ' young Doc Smythe looked surprised; he had not really noticed it, having been born into it – 'in which one bellowing father more or less is a mere nothing. Just a fact of life.'

'So if I can keep the kid alive he'll be OK.'

'That's our job, keeping 'em alive. It's not for us to say whether he has the brains or the courage to become what you call OK. But to keep the body alive and functioning, growing and putting on weight (until the time comes when it's necessary to take weight *off*, of course), that's our work. It sounds straightforward, elementary even, but it's not so damned easy, is it?'

The young doc eyed the old doc with a new respect. Here was a man with a sense of proportion and a sense of humour – were they perhaps one and the same, or very closely connected?

14
Local Government

'Luv,' said Clara Howlett to her husband, 'there's going to be a vacancy on the Parish Council, and you know how it is now, after Reorganization: the District Council's a joke because its district is too big, and the County Council's a worse joke because its County is far too big, but the Parish Councils have come into their own.'

'What's all this about?'

'Old man Spink's gone off to hospital, and not likely to come out, the word is.'

'Ought to have been put off the Council years ago under the age rule anyway,' said Howlett.

'Oh, they don't do that sort of thing in the country,' said Clara, 'not unless there's a lucky break like taking some old codger off to hospital or burying him. But it's happened here and there'll be a vacancy.'

'What about it?'

'Why don't you stand?'

'Clara duck, I've quitted the arena, I've killed my bulls and not much gain of it. I mean, the strike at Fellowses' and the strike at Cowie's, hard times, hard words, and we *won* – a few extra pounds a week, but today the pounds have turned into pennies.'

'That's time catching up with you. Whatever anyone, boss or shop-steward or whoever, thinks he's pulled off, time catches up and makes it a nonsense. But there has been a step taken. It all goes forward just that bit. Someone has to take steps.'

'Grandmother's Steps,' said Howlett, naming a children's game which he and Clara had played at Infant School.

Clara laughed, they both laughed, but the vacancy on the Parish Council was not forgotten by Clara. Howlett had no intention of standing, if only because his neighbour the Brig was chairman and would certainly shoot him 'for real' if he came out into the open. Clara laughed at this notion. 'After the Court case, everyone would spot him as the murderer. He'd never try it on. You'd be safer on the Parish Council than in our bed, luv.'

'But I don't *want* – '

'Look, your lovely bit of garden isn't a farm, it isn't a life-work when you're only sixty-five. You can't just opt out of living to *cultiver* your *jardin* – '

'Clara, I know you were a school-teacher when I stole you away – '

'And you are quite educated enough to translate two words of French. I can think of some more, English poetry, but I can only remember my private version: "Ten thousand times I've washed and dressed, And done my teeth and changed my vest, And all's to do again." Time always catches up with you, it's always all to do again, *but someone's got to do it.*'

'It doesn't have to be me. And there's another thing, we are newcomers. I bet there's already a local chap lined up for the vacant place. You're nobody round here unless your grand-dad was buddies with someone else's grand-dad. It's not like the big cities where people come and go. Here, they don't go. Any incomer is a stranger for fifty years. So no hope for me. I'll have changed my vest for the last time before I'm a hundred and fifteen!'

More laughter.

But Clara knew and her husband knew that his conscience, his curse, had been stirred. It had always been his bane; without it he would never have become a shop-steward, and with it he had had a hard time as a shop-steward, trying to sort out the genuine chaps from the yobbos: all of them *men* in the sense of Union membership, but not all of them worth the name in any other sense.

Now, surely, his damned conscience, having done its work until his retirement, would leave him alone?

'Clara, what's bothering you exactly?' he demanded one day.

'Well, I dare say you don't know because you never even walk across the Green, the place is becoming a dump. There was a pond – now full of old fridges and washing-machines. And the courting couples who come in cars after dark, they leave not only showers of Kleenex, beer-cans, crisp-packets, but other things I'd blush to mention except to you. *Festoons* of french letters and torn panties on the gorse-bushes.'

'Where do they come from?'

'Radmere's a baby city now, new houses taking in at least three villages. Light-industry. The rubbish comes in cars: they don't carry it by hand, do they?'

'So what?'

'We need a bye-law like the other commons have, Bartham Great Common, Bruton Ling, places where people like to take kids and dogs for a run-around in fresh air. There's a surprising lot of commons round here and I can tell you why if you're interested.'

'Carry on, schoolmarm.'

'Because so much of the land is sandy and stony. OK for village grazing but not worth enclosing and ploughing up, high times or low times, not even in the Napoleonic Wars. So we've got commons, and bloody common people spoiling them.'

'Go on.'

'A bye-law against motor vehicles can be got from the Home Secretary by a Parish Council, that's the starter.'

'How the hell do *you* know?'

'From one of the old dears at the Flower Club, a common-right owner at Bruton. They've got a bye-law and notices stuck around which people don't read, so she toddles round and politely asks drivers to move to five yards (I think) off the public road.'

'And nobody's beaten her up yet?'

'She was threatened with a big stick by a big lunatic the other day, but she has a big stick herself because of a bad hip. He was led away, shouting, by some woman, wife or keeper.'

'Your Flower Club lady must be quite a girl.'

'A very old girl and not at all good at flower-arranging. Her thing seems to have been fighting, like yours. See a wrong and try to right it.'

Silence.

Clara went on, 'If nobody on this Parish Council cares, our Green will be one great stinking rubbish-dump.'

Silence.

'And it's not as though the dustmen won't remove our big stuff: they will, if tipped, and why shouldn't they be tipped for heavy lifting?'

Silence.

'But that won't prevent the small disgustings being chucked out all over the Green from cars by people who won't take their disgustings home in paper bags to their own dustbins.'

'Clara, love, does it really *matter*?'

'It matters unless you've got a deaf nose and blind eyes. Last week, bags of stinking dead chickens were dumped. I think they died on their ghastly journey from the loathsome hatchery at Budgrave to the so-called factory at Radmere. Anyway, there they still are, reeking among the old prams and whatnots. A horrid sight and a far worse smell in a public place. Wrong, isn't it? Time was, when you saw something wrong, you tried to change it. Time was.'

'But we are strangers here.'

And he was right. The vacancy on the Parish Council was filled by an ancient with poor eyesight and no sense of smell, whose ancestors had farmed, from the year dot, the land on which he still had a house, but which he no longer farmed.

Howlett obtained only four votes.

'Well, that's it, Clara, I'm not making myself a cockshy again.'

'Next time, the village will know us better. We won't be strangers for ever.'

'Till death we will. Of course we'll have impressive funerals, everyone will come, they love funerals. But it'll be too late then.'

Laughter. The Howletts were good at laughing. Their earlier life had been hard, so they had learned to laugh when they could. And the hairy dog always came bounding up to laugh with them.

The Radmere Town Council, demoted under the Reorganization from Urban District Council to a body with a much smaller area to look after and much less money with which to look after it, suffered, that autumn, an attack in the local Press, mainly from old people, because of the dreadful state of the pavements; these pavements were made of large stone slabs, much broken because heavy vehicles climbed up on them in order to pass one another: and the broken pieces stuck up and stubbed the toes of old people, few of whom lifted their feet as smartly as they had done when young. So the old, and not only the old, fell on their faces on the pavements of Radmere; for when one is walking forwards, whether one is old or young, a sharp stub of a toe causes one to *fall* forwards.

Harriet Brandling wrote:

One has to look at one's feet all the time: this means one bumps into other people, and never recognizes friend or foe. I measured my length in an unexpected place the other day, where the pavement was wide – but very uneven. Luckily I have learnt, from riding and skating, how to fall, and all I had was bruises. But one day an old person will fall and break a thigh, and will die in hospital of hypostatic pneumonia, which is what old people get when suddenly immobilized. And the Radmere Town Council, whether charged with it or not, will be guilty of manslaughter.

Not one to mince her words, Harriet Brandling. Her trade was words.

The other complainants, all of whom had at one time or another, in one street or another, tripped and fallen because of up-jutting bits of pavement, were less outspoken than Harriet, but their letters made an impressive column.

In the next issue of both local weeklies, a Councillor made a reply, to the effect that the cost of buying large granite paving-stones and re-laying about a mile of broken pavement would be prohibitive and besides, as soon as it was done, two lorries trying to pass one another in any of the narrow streets would break up the new paving as they had done the old. And the Conservationists, for whom the writer clearly had a strong dislike, were united against the cheaper attempt at improvement, namely tarmac pavements, easily made and repaired.

The following week, Harriet leapt in again. All the narrow streets should be made into one-way streets, so no vehicle would ever be compelled to climb on to a pavement. But the pavements on the wider streets were just as bad, as she had pointed out a fortnight previously, and for her part, since she did not look at her feet all the time, she would see little aesthetic difference between granite slabs and tarmac. What, exactly, were pavements *for*? For people to walk on, or for Conservationists to slap Conservation-orders on?

Short and to the point, as usual.

'I do hate that old woman,' a youngish Councillor unwisely said. 'Always poking her nose in, doesn't even live in the town, not one of *our* ratepayers.'

An older Councillor said, 'This is her shopping-town, it has to be, as for countless others who aren't *our* ratepayers. If they stopped shopping here, you and I, James, would have to shut up shop: this totty little town by itself wouldn't support us, in the style to which we have become accustomed – we don't live above our shops any more, as my parents did and yours – we have nice houses in the country and motorcars to bring us to Radmere every day. We need customers. Mrs Brandling is a customer, and a good one, because she's too old to be dashing off to Norwich or Ipswich or Bury. If you think about *that*, the personal thing will hit you much harder than the rates thing. We really ought to try to make life safer for the dozens, the hundreds of Mrs Brandlings who provide us with our living.'

'Re-paving the pavements with big granite pavements is too madly expensive,' said a woman Councillor.

'Abso-bally-lutely,' said the Chairman, a man of middle age, a bit out of date with his slang, 'so we might consider the other thing, tarmac pavement. Would they ruin our town?'

'How much do lovers of landscape or architecture, or both, look at their feet?' said the woman Councillor. 'Very seldom, I'd say. So if we keep these uneven old stone pavements we are benefiting nobody and might easily kill somebody, for the sake of a small band of people who want everything to go on exactly as it did in the Year Dot. I'm for tarmac pavements.'

The Press was not admitted to Council meetings, but it waited outside. Both the lads surged up to the departing Councillors, notebooks at the ready, with the same question – the only question of truly local concern – 'Was there anything about the pavements?'

'Nothing definite,' the Chairman said repressively. 'The question of expense is a grave one, and we should have to consider estimates, whatever course we decided to pursue.'

'But you do mean to do *something*?'

'If we can budget for it,' said the Chairman dismissively.

But the woman Councillor, and one of the men, felt that the town's business ought to be done as openly as possible. Each was nobbled by one of the lads. But it so happened that, though both in favour of openness, they differed about the pavements. The she-Councillor said tarmac seemed the practical and least expensive answer, the man said it would be dreadful to deface their ancient town by tarmac pavements. So after the next issue of both papers, the controversy went on raging wildly. This was good for the circulation of the papers; the boys knew they had done well.

'But nothing *happens*,' wailed Aubrey Stiff, the blood-thirsty one.

'Something will happen if some old person breaks a thigh and dies of it, like that militant female said in her first letter. If that's what you want you'll maybe get it,' said Colin Crisp. 'I don't really want it, not even for a scoop.'

'I sometimes think you haven't got journalists' blood in your veins. You're too patient, and you never will try to stir things up *yourself.*'

'Things you and I stir up wouldn't be news. A stone chucked into a muddy pond gets nothing out but a lot of ripples and maybe a haapin'-tood.'

'And what the hell's that?'

'A frog, laddie, a toad that hops instead of shambling. Give an ear to the dialect if you want to understand what witnesses say to you. This stuff we have round here is a very strong dialect, as foreign as Northumbrian to educated Southerners like you. I can't take Northumbrian – on the Telly, you know – unless they'll speak slowly. It's the vowels that are different. And the same with Norfolk and Suffolk, though *they* aren't identical, worse luck. You have to tune your ears, or you'll make no end of silly mistakes. What could a haapin'-tood be if not a hopping-toad? I tremble to think of the mess you'd make of the evidence of eyewitnesses in any of the accidents or man-slaughters you long for, if you can't understand the lingo.'

'Thanks for the lecture, Uncle,' said Aubrey sourly.

'Don't mention it. And for a bonus you could try to get an interview with that first old dame. She does speak English.'

'But she's written her bit *twice.*'

'She could write a whole lot more if she cared to, and they'd print it. She's not just any old woman.'

'I'd never heard of her.'

'That doesn't surprise me. Look her up in OOZOO in the Library. And remember, a prophet is not without honour, save in his own country and among his own people. (Bible – if you've heard of *that* before.) She's identified round here with the agricultural non-culture, having been a farmer's wife and cook and factotum for donkey's years – '

'What do you mean, agricultural non-culture, big-head? I've an uncle who's a very important farmer, you hear him on the morning radio all the time – '

'And how's his culture? Can he tell you who Palestrina was, or Blake or Swift or Beardsley?'

Aubrey Stiff bristled. 'Why should he? Are they anything to do with farming?'

'One of them, rather notably though briefly. All of them should have been heard of by educated people. Like us. You and I are supposed to be literate, that's how we earn our living. What painters do you know?'

'Munnings,' said Aubrey.

'Musicians?'

'Somebody Britten.'

'Poets?'

'I've never been one for that sort of rubbish. Wasn't there a Lord Someone?'

'More than one. You ought to be a farmer's boy-hoy-hoy, laddie, not a journalist. It would have suited you better, more eventful.'

'*More eventful?*'

'Disasters all the time. The farmer will never be happy again, he carries his heart in his boots, For either the rain is destroying his grain, Or the drought is destroying his roots. There's poetry for you: can't guarantee an absolutely accurate quotation, but the sense is there. Crisis upon crisis even if you don't get swine-fever or foot-and-mouth or anthrax. You'd be happier working for your uncle than trying to find events in the catchment area of the Radmere Weekly News.'

'My pa would ask me what my expensive education was for.'

'That's what I ask myself also, bor. School-fees don't do

much good if the brains aren't there. What have you learnt
except to speak standard English and despise local dialects?'

'I can play squash and tennis and rugger . . . and cricket'
(on a dying fall).

'So useful, when your chosen trade is the written word.'

'D'you know, I hate your guts,' said Aubrey to Colin.

'I don't hate yours,' said Colin to Aubrey, 'I just wish you
had some. Patience, perseverance against boredom, deter-
mination to learn to spell and to win the battle against
English grammar: those are guts, in our profession.'

Hubert Carlyon rode a stationary bicycle in his basement.
A man of his standing could not be seen riding a bicycle
in the streets like any workman (it had not yet filtered
through his thick layer of class-consciousness that more than
half the workmen who had work also had motor-cars) and
certainly could not be seen walking more than a few steps.
But he had always been haunted by a bulge in the belly and
as he grew older it grew larger, so he kept a captive bicycle in
the basement, on which he rode – he told his wife – thirty
miles a day to keep himself in trim.

She said, 'If you rode thirty miles out of doors, you'd get
to see a whole lot of interesting and beautiful places. I
wish I could, but my range is limited to about five at most
because of the cooking and cleaning.'

'I'm not interested in the local landscape,' said Hubert.
'I'm interested in keeping fit.'

'For what?' asked Alice. 'You've never done anything
but sedentary work. Are you contemplating getting down to
real work, but where, but how?'

'You bloody idiot,' said Carlyon, an address to his wife
which was so common as to pass unnoticed, 'I just want to
take exercise for my health.'

'And what will you use your health for?' asked Alice.

'Gainful employment, or just golf?'

'Just golf, dear wife and helpmeet, since we no longer have to pay school-fees for your ghastly offspring.'

'He's yours too, remember.'

'How do I know?'

'You silly old ass, he arrived ten months after you got home from that posting. *Ten* months. And you never saw any males hanging round me; if you had, you'd have shot 'em. That's what you said from the very day we were married; I took it as a compliment at first and I'm not so madly sexy anyway.'

'You can say that again!' he spat out, and went down to the basement.

The too-dry spell of weather had broken up into a too-wet spell. An autumn of splendid colour, unobserved by Carlyon, had become an autumn of heavy rain in which only the tenacious leaves of oak gave a hint of orange splendour in the gloom. If Carlyon had gone out of doors (which he never did unless someone's car picked him up for golf) he would have found a long shallow lake outside the terrace of ugly houses. In his basement, bicycling away without getting anywhere, he suddenly felt icy feet. In the poor light of the forty-watt bulb, he saw water instead of brick floor, and his pedals began to splash on the down-stroke. He jumped off his machine into at least a foot of water, and rushed up the short flight of stairs into the kitchen, bellowing for his wife. He wore a T-shirt, tight red shorts, ankle socks and plimsolls, and revealed great thick hairy legs all the way up from socks to the crease of the buttocks. When this vision slopped into the kitchen making wet footmarks on the floor, Alice took one look, choked, spluttered, and burst out laughing in spite of all her efforts at control.

'Damn you, woman,' he yelled, 'it's no laughing matter –

we're flooded in the basement.'

'I was sure we would be,' she said.

'*What?*'

'All the houses in this terrace get flooded, that's why the basements have never been used for what they were built for, kitchens and larders and servants. Everything's had to go one floor up, so we have a nice light kitchen: suits me – '

'But you never *told* me.'

'It's no good ever telling you anything, dear, because you don't listen. The house-agents are the ones who should have told you, but one can see why they didn't: they weren't asked.'

'Damn' dishonest. Actionable.'

'I doubt it. They told no lie. We could have thought of it ourselves, or asked someone, seeing that this bottom side of the town is at river level so the basements are probably below it. In very wet weather like this – '

'The blasted Town Council ought to clear out the storm-drains.'

'But where would the water go if they did, the river being too full to take it? It seeps back to the lowest level it can find, these basements.'

'And how does it get in?'

'Filters through the soil and the bricks, I suppose: it's sandy soil, you know.'

'You bloody woman, *you don't mind*!'

'Not really. The house is big enough for us without a basement.'

'But my bike. You could have told me, and I'd never have fixed my bike down there.'

'You don't imagine I wanted it in my kitchen, do you? Why can't you ride a real bicycle out of doors or just walk on foot if you need exercise? Your silly captive bicycle is just an excuse. Who knows if you do the thirty miles a day you say you do? There's no difference in your shape.'

He emitted a sort of roar and took three steps towards her. She held up both hands in a 'stop' gesture. 'Hit me,' she said, 'and it's the police, and you cease to be a gentleman. The papers will love it.'

That cowed him. He was paying heavily for his one and only attempt. He asked her to get him some dry socks and slippers: that was something even the most uppity wife would surely do.

'I will, also trousers. You should see yourself in those shortie shorties,' said Alice.

'You're no oil-painting yourself in that greasy overall, with your hair like a bird's nest,' said Carlyon.

'Fair enough,' said Alice, annoying him far more by calmness than she would have done by temper. If only she would swear and shout, if only she'd cry! Crying was what proper women did. Instead of crying, she equably explained, 'I've been doing out the oven, a messy job, and I do wish they'd make ovens a bit higher off the floor.'

'For heaven's sake stop nattering about trifles. Get my dry things and then go and look at the flood.'

When Alice peered down into the dim-lit basement, she saw the seat of the bicycle sticking up out of the water like the rump of a drowned animal. The dark unrippling flood must, she guessed, be three feet deep and rising. But it would not rise much more, the neighbours had said, and would soon ebb after the rain stopped. It was a matter of no moment to Alice, who, naturally, had never used the basement for anything. She said to herself, 'I might have told him before he fixed his silly bike down there, but I just forgot. I have everything to think of, the meals, the washing, the washing-up, the sweeping and dusting and Charlie – I have to watch Charlie, though he seems happy at school now, because he's still so skinny.'

'Well,' demanded Carlyon when she shut the basement door.

'It won't get much higher and will go down quickly when the rain stops. It was stupid to make basements in houses down here at the bottom of the town, but no doubt no one in 1850 conceived of a town house without a basement.'

'Well, I'm going to get some action,' said Carlyon. 'I'm going to sue the Town Council.'

'Good luck to you. It'll give you something to do anyway,' said Alice, and went back to her oven.

'God, how I hate you,' he hissed through clenched teeth. But he wasn't going to raise his hand to her again, whatever happened.

Life was indeed pleasanter while he was rousing the other five families; Alice saw less of him. Six angry letters appeared in due course in both the strictly local papers. The Chairman of the Town Council replied that the Council had neither built the houses nor ordered the rain; the Council could not be blamed for the failure of the purchasers to have their properties surveyed.

Six more letters, the following week, took varied lines; two said the storm-drains were inadequate, this being Town Council work, two said that honest house-agents ought not to need checking by surveyors and two others said that since their rates included drainage they were not going to pay and would go to prison first.

The young reporters, waiting on the side-lines, all agog, weighed in, having now three sets of people, not only the obstinately mum Town Council, to interview. To Carlyon, the fragmentation of his campaign was not good – he wanted damages, he wanted money – but to Colin and Aubrey it was a boon. From all this lot, somebody would cough up something which might make the National Press, the goal of every country reporter.

Those who said they would go to prison rather than pay rates looked the best bet to Aubrey, but Colin disillusioned him. 'They wouldn't. They are both fathers of families, their wives wouldn't let 'em. The only people who go to jug for their principles are the single, without responsibilities, and good luck to them but they aren't all that numerous. You should go for the people who want money out of this mess. Try the ones who are gunning for the house-agents: find out *which* house-agents, and grill them too.'

'And what about you?'

'Carlyon and his next-door-but-one who have it in for the Council about the storm-drains. Mind you, I've been generous to you, kid. Your line might go on for ages, appeal to the High Court if you're lucky. Mine will peter out. There is *no* action against the Town Council. Nothing they could do would stop the water-table rising in a wet time, or prevent water finding its own level.'

'How about deepening the river? It's not much more than a stream.'

'That's not Town Council business. The far bigger Water Authority would have to do it, and I don't see 'em, not for a totty little town like Radmere. You see, deepening a river has to be from the mouth upwards, else you only create floods somewhere else. Why, for the useless basements of six houses in Radmere, should the Water Board deepen the river right down to the sea?'

'Where do you get all that stuff from, Colin?'

'I learnt about the water-table in Geography at Grammar School, free gratis and for nothing. While you were memorizing counties and capitals, situated on rivers, and capes and bays and all that jazz, at great expense. Names are nothing, laddie, the facts underneath the names are all.'

But while the two boys were pursuing their inquiries as well as they could, something else happened, an echo from an earlier protest, that of the old girls who had wailed about the uneven pavement. Old Mrs Brandling stubbed her toe and fell, broke her thigh and could not rise again, and was taken off in an ambulance to the N. and N. hospital. It was by sheer luck and not any devotion to the care of the sick on the part of the doctors, on half-way strike that autumn, that Harriet Brandling was admitted. She had with her, however, the necessary documents about the destination of her body, having been perfectly conscious though in great pain when picked up by the police in Main Street, Radmere. Her last intelligible words in hospital, where her broken bone showed no signs of mending, were to her visiting friend Jane Peters:

'How lucky that you are with us, Janey. You can cook for poor old Harold until the children find a Home for him.'

'Oh Harriet, I'll look after him till you get back.'

'I'll not get back. Not at eighty. This is the last of me, and no regrets. I've seen you right in a codicil to my Will, and the children will do the best they can for Harold except coping with him themselves; they all have their own problems. The days of man's years are threescore years and ten. If we insist on living longer, we have to take the consequences. Labour and sorrow, labour and sorrow.'

Her voice trailed away; she was under strong sedation and on the verge of sleep. Janey Peters left, in tears. Nobody but the hospital staff saw Harriet again; after the blood-clot rose to her lung and stayed there she was soon and quietly dead and a plain van came from Cambridge to fetch her corpse.

Everybody in the Radmere catchment area was surprised to see that Harriet had quite a long and laudatory obituary in *The Times*. They had had no idea. A prophet is not without honour save in his own country and among his own people. But while the generality were 'whoolly stammed', the two young reporters were jubilant. Here at last was an event. A death, and no natural death. A death caused by the rotten pavements of Radmere.

Harold Brandling did not even know Harriet had gone. He still had a woman in the house, to provide him with food, and the only other things he wanted were television and sleep. The reporters came to interview him, separately, and both soon realized that he did not know what they were talking about. Disappointed, they decided that *that* old codger was not likely to take action against the Council.

But the Council knew it had killed Harriet Brandling, and started hacking up the broken pavements a week after her death. A world-respected author of historical studies, she had not died in vain. The pavements of a tin-pot little town would be the safer for the sacrifice of her life.

But it was another non-event for the young reporters. No one was going to charge the Town Council with murder or man-slaughter, nor even sue it for damages; least of all the dead old woman's very old husband who did not know or care what had happened. And the re-making of the pavements stopped after about fifty yards. The Council could afford no more.

15
Farewells

So Harriet Brandling's by no means wholly natural death sparked off nothing, not even a further outbreak of letters to the local papers. Her old contemporaries had had their say and could not be bothered to write again. There was all the worry of Christmas ahead, everything so expensive, including postage-stamps. Harriet was not mourned by any but her own children. Her friends took the line which she herself would have taken: she had had a long innings and a good one, and none of us lives for ever.

The two reporter-lads could elicit nothing for their papers. The readers of the national dailies had learned that someone of a certain limited distinction had departed, but that was not the kind of thing which interested the two strictly local weeklies. Had Harriet been a film-star, a Miss England or a murderess, *that* would have been a boost for the readers: 'I knew her', 'I often saw her in the town',

'She used to talk to me about my dog': a vicarious distinction would have been conferred on anyone who had seen her around, had she been a film-star, a Miss England or a murderess. But she had even cheated the locals of a funeral. She had been carted off to Cambridge in a plain van.

And within days the flood in the basements of Victoria Terrace had dwindled away too, because the rain had ceased and the river itself had dwindled into its proper channel, where it resumed its customary almost invisible flow. The only person still maintaining a high state of rage in Victoria Terrace was the man Carlyon, on account of his bicycle. He, however, dared not move against the Council if he alone had to risk the costs of an action, so another promising rumpus had fizzled out.

The schools too seemed to be muddling along without providing news. There might possibly be something worth hearing on Speech Day if one could keep alert through the speechifying.

In early December, both the young reporters suffered from shock. They met on a country road, each in a motor-car. Aubrey had a camera-man with him and a label on the windscreen which said PRESS, while Colin was on his own in a battered old car with a similar PRESS label on the windscreen. They hooted at each other and halted.

'Cor, what's happened to you?' asked Colin.

'You could call it promotion. Old Wilkins has retired, so I have his down-river assignment, but I haven't passed my test yet so Bill has to come with me, and it works out very well. Bill, this is Colin, our rival.'

Bill showed no rancour towards a rival.

'So what about you?' asked Aubrey.

'You could call it promotion. Ben Coe has died and I've got his catchment area and his car, and I don't need company because I've a driving licence,' said Colin.

'Where are you going?'

'Same place as you. Nativity Play at Stonebrook Comprehensive Junior or Junior Comprehensive, whatever they call it – the bottom end of that enormous school at the far end of our beat.'

The large and mostly parental audience of the Nativity Play seemed to enjoy it, but the reporter-boys had had so many, even at their tender age, to sit through (and even to act in, during their schooldays) that they were bored. It was, after all, impossible to present a highly original Nativity Play: author and producer dared not depart far from the text.

Colin said to Aubrey, 'Praise is obligatory. It was certainly pretty.'

Aubrey said, 'It's a way of teaching kids to stand up, speak up and shut up. That's what school plays are for.'

'And who are you selecting for special commendation? We have to name names,' said Colin.

'The Holy Child was OK because it was a doll,' said Aubrey. 'And you could say Joseph was very natural because he looked as if the whole thing stank. I bet it did in real life too, if it ever happened. One could write a novel about Joseph, the most neglected character in the whole legend.'

'One could indeed, if one had seventy-five thousand words in one's locker,' said Colin. 'Why don't you? It's the best idea I've heard for ages. What did he think of all that about Angels and the Holy Ghost? Whatever the facts of the case, seeing how badly the Jews needed a star in the sky it might look good to be the foster-father of the Son of God,' said Colin. 'There's a lot of possible angles.'

'But as of now, as they say, and I hope we don't say, what can we write about that play, so very like every other Nativity Play?'

'You're all right, you've got your camera-man. You'll

need nothing but a caption,' said Colin. 'I've no picture so I must churn out some words,' and he departed in haste.

Ten minutes later, Aubrey and the camera-man came upon him by the roadside, kicking and swearing at the elderly car he had inherited from the late Ben Coe. They pulled up.

'Something wrong?'

'Everything's been wrong since I took over this bag of tricks. Four punctures. Well, the paper pays. But *this* means I can't get home. It's not a wheel. The clutch has burnt out. I thought I smelt a smell, but you do get smells in old cars.'

'Wow,' said Aubrey, 'pity I hadn't some wonderful scoop to beat you with. But there aren't any wonderful scoops round here. Hop in. We'll take you back to Radmere since there's no scoop.'

Colin gave a final kick to the old car before shoving it on to the grass verge, a heavy task which led him to observe, 'If there's one thing more maddening than another, it's machinery which doesn't work. My kingdom for a horse!' He then fitted himself into the back of Aubrey's car along with the photographic junk.

'What we suffer, in such piffling causes,' remarked Aubrey over his shoulder to his passenger.

'School plays aren't piffling to the actors and their mums and occasionally dads,' said Colin. 'Our readers, boy.'

'Well, I can tell you I'm not sticking it much longer. I want to be where the action is, and it isn't here.'

'Well, where?'

'You *must* have heard of Belfast. Or even London or Brum would do.'

'Fancy yourself as a War Correspondent? You wouldn't get that title, you know. It's not war, it 'ud be more decent if it was.'

'I know, but I might *deserve* the title. All you deserve here is a putty medal for endurance.'

In due course they wrote their reports of the Nativity Play and Colin's paper bought a picture from Aubrey's photographer. There was not even any competition. It was as dull as that.

The next thing was the Speech Day at the Grammar School, which did set some cats among some pigeons. The report presented by Old Grey Boss said plainly that Parents' Choice had produced a real mess of overcrowding and teachers' despair. He could have said, quite shortly, that parents hadn't a clue, which was what he meant, but he dared not be as rude as all that. So what he said was that there could be no more Parents' Choice for his school, there would be highly selective entrance upon the best recommendations of Middle School headmasters. Only the top children, academically, could be selected, because of the gross overcrowding caused by Parents' Choice. That put parents where they belonged, said Colin to himself. Ambitious idiots. No grasp of abilities or potentials. Just a step up the social ladder for my kid.

These manifestations of real life in the catchment area interested Colin more and more as he learned more about them. The country – defiled commons, disputed footpaths, bad pavements, educational economies and muddles, even speechifying about all these things – was more endurable, the more one understood about what made people tick. They did tick, even in outlying farm cottages they went on ticking. Young Aubrey, on the other hand, would have preferred people to stop ticking, through some act of violence, for choice. He had not identified himself with the Radmere catchment area at all. He thirsted for crises and blood: anything that would save him from filling space over and over again with the same old words about the same old non-events, and mostly long lists of the same old names at that.

How Colin could be so unambitious as to contemplate staying on in the area, Aubrey could not imagine. Colin had said something about not growing unless you had roots. Aubrey riposted, 'Maybe, but why here?' To which Colin answered that the country was the only place where there was room for roots. Aubrey muttered, but to himself, 'Too much room.' He had not found out anything about the seemingly unoccupied acres and acres which produced the food he ate. The country, to him, was still a nearly empty place dotted with very small villages, and market-towns unworthy of the name of Town. Nobody would plant bombs in the Radmere pubs.

The most that happened was a few drunken yobs burgling shops, and if they pleaded drunkenness they got off lightly, to the disgust not only of the young policeman who caught them but of Aubrey Stiff also. Drunks were run-of-the-mill, they did not rate headlines. There seemed to be nobody in the catchment area running wild on hard drugs. A pity. Horse would have made headlines.

The young policeman's view was from a different angle, burglary was burglary and drunkenness was no excuse for *anything*, burglary, GBH, murder on the roads or baby-battering. The excesses committed under the influence of one drug were no more excusable than those committed under the influence of another. Crime was crime.

Christmas hove into view. Next year stood back in the wings, waiting. Aubrey Stiff was tired of waiting. His father, pleased that the boy had more guts than had been hitherto apparent, pulled a string or two and manoeuvred him into Belfast as correspondent to a Midland weekly not unlike the one he was leaving behind in East Anglia. The pay was slightly better, but Aubrey's father was less keen on the pay than on proving that his son would one day become a man, even in the profession he had so oddly chosen.

So Aubrey missed a thing which happened on the last day of the Suffolk schools' term and which made the National headlines.

The Dickin children were bicycling from the parsonage at Forde to their school at Castle Eyot: and the Christmas traffic on the main road – which was a mere road, not a motorway – was building up. Mammoth lorries carrying all kinds of goods to Norwich and beyond thundered in from the coast for the Christmas trade. The clever, confident little Dickin girl was killed because one mammoth vehicle swung widely out to pass another just at the crossroads, at high speed and with no indication of intention.

The Coroner's verdict had to be Accidental Death, since his Court was not a place of trial. But on the statements given to the police by the only two witnesses, the other driver and the shocked little Dickin brother, it was clear that the slayer ought to come before another Court if the Law could catch up with him. Colin Crisp was at the inquest and learned from the evidence of the father, who seemed to have his emotions well under control, that the dead child had been thoroughly instructed at school in road safety and had survived the hazards of the main road for more than two years, therefore it was highly unlikely that the fault was hers.

A few days, too few days, later, Colin was sent to Forde Rectory to interview the parents. The National papers had already given a paragraph or two to the sad event but the local papers (he was temporarily acting for both) wanted something less impersonal and much longer.

Alan Dickin, that solid, self-controlled man, opened the door to Colin and would have shut it again when Colin named his newspaper, but already a tall, gaunt and hollow-eyed woman who was probably Mrs Dickin stood behind her husband and said, 'Bring him in, Alan. Why should we not talk to the Press? There's nothing secret about our little girl's death.'

So the three of them went into a pleasant sitting-room. The little boy was not there. 'He's gone to some cousins in Essex, great friends they are,' explained the Reverend. 'He'll forget before long.'

When they were settled with cigarettes, Colin said to the Reverend in the crass way interviewers have of asking umbrella questions, the answers to which would fill several volumes, 'What are your feelings about this terrible tragedy?' It was what he had been told to find out but even as he said the words he heard how stupid they were.

Alan Dickin, however, answered promptly and briefly.

'I keep in mind that the Lord giveth and the Lord taketh away. Blessèd be the name of the Lord.'

Golly, thought Colin. And someone else thought Golly too.

'If you say that again I'll leave you,' said Helen Dickin through her teeth.

'But our child is at peace, dear. No more harm can come to her. There's a lot of harm in this world which might have come to her.'

'What child wants peace? What adult with a grain of sense wants peace – at any price, the price of rotten big lorries, the price of life? These are not the times for rabbiting on about peace. It was more peaceful in the war. When people got killed we did know what it was supposed to be *for*. The word was Freedom. But what has Jenny been killed for, what's the word today? I'll tell you – no one else will. Money. Stinking lorries rushing along the roads to make money for stinking business-men. And our little girl, with such an interesting life before her, is dead in the scramble for money. Put that in God's pipe and let him smoke it.'

'My dear, we have a stranger with us. You mustn't talk like that. Will you please go, Mr Er. My wife is naturally distressed. Your paper ought not to have sent you to us so soon, if ever.'

Colin mumbled something and went, his brain seething with the abundance of information about reality which had been poured into it. He had gone to the Rectory in an enterprising mood, knowing that anything about the clergy was good for a headline: and he had been bowled over as by a tidal wave. Talk about a scoop! But of course he could not use it. No decent person could transcribe that dialogue for the public to read. After Helen Dickin's first sentence he had stopped writing. Now though he could have written it all practically verbatim, he knew he would have to boil it down to a paragraph about lorries which were too big for the roads, and *that* was no longer news.

But he felt enriched, in a melancholy way; he could store up this experience and feel his way into it as though the tragedy had struck his own trivial young life. I'll be a novelist, he thought. I'll beat young Aubrey and his Joseph to the post.

In which he was right, for young Aubrey was killed in a pub-bombing before the end of the month.

Christmas rolled up, a four-day holiday, a bad time for all newspapers, not only the locals. Readers had gone to ground in family enclaves, the accident of date made it impossible for the locals to be published on the proper day, and what was there in the way of news anyway? The Nationals, in their scant appearances before New Year, would merely be recapping past events, the choice of top books, films, plays, personalities; together with purely theoretic forecasts about the year to come. The nitty-gritty locals had no top books, films, plays or personalities to record, and any events which could be called events were mostly sad ones, best not recorded. Births and marriages were not events, they were an epidemic, and deaths were supposed to be sad even when they weren't. Colin dug up two golden weddings and a diamond, not clear whether these were occasions for congratulation or commiseration.

At Christmas, Hubert Carlyon spent a great deal of time on the golf-course and at the nineteenth hole. He enjoyed his Christmas because that was the proper thing. At home he was by turns more genial and more foul, according to the amount of refreshment to which he was treated at the clubhouse. He never paid for more than one round himself. He couldn't, without cutting down on Alice's housekeeping money – and that would have repercussed against his own stomach in the following week. His wife, son and daughter had a quietly jolly time while he was out. The daughter was good at entertaining her young brother, having chosen to be a teacher because she liked to help young minds along.

But when Father came home with too much to carry, he made caustic remarks about the daughter who taught the polloi what the polloi were better without, and shouted at his wife because poor Charlie, not so very bright, his spell at prep-school having been constantly interrupted by illness, would have to go to the yob-school (Carlyon's phrase) now that Parents' Choice had been revoked. All Alice's doing. *His* son, destined to make the wrong friends and end up working at petrol-pumps or suchlike. So it was a patchy Christmas for the Carlyons, alternating between quiet fun and loud shouting-matches. Alice and her children went to church for carols. Church was not a habit of hers, but it was a place where Hubert could not come bursting in.

At Willington Green nobody felt they ought to go to church because the House of God, like the house meant for the parson, was disused. The church of the next parish was not far away but there was no obligation to attend it. Years before, when Willington Green had a Rector and a usable church, Brigadier Gault had been Rector's Warden, therefore in duty bound to attend all services, and Irene his wife had gladly accompanied him in order to have a time of peace and contemplation and maybe prayer, though she was never sure what happened to prayers. Nobody, from childhood onwards, had answered her prayer to have a dog of her own.

And now that the seasons and feasts of the church had left Willington Green, the Brigadier was high and dry and so was Irene. It never occurred to the Brig to take out his motorcar and drive to the next parish for the festivals of Christianity – he was not Rector's Warden but a nobody, in the next parish. The Gault's Christmas consisted of a large ill-cooked meal and a lot of indigestion.

Their neighbours the Howletts had no indigestion, though, like the Gaults, they had no religion either. They rose late, ate well, exercised the hairy dog, took a few looks at television, and read books given to them by their children. Reading books was a very rare activity in Willington Green, where 'book' meant any kind of magazine including the BBC and ITV output of programmes. The books given to the Howletts by their children were about architecture and cooking, suitable interests for the elderly who had retired from the arena. The Howletts were pleased to discover that some famous architecture was within range of Willington Green. 'We'll go and see some of these places when the days get longer,' said Howlett.

On the evening of Boxing Day there was a quiet and only slightly alcoholic party at Deanery House in Radmere. Harold Brandling was now a resident, and so, thanks to the departure to hospital of another old cove, was Janey Peters, enabled to pay the fees by the provisions of Harriet's Will. She was a great help to Harold because he knew her and she

knew several of the other old people. She could not tell
whether he had succeeded in sorting them out, but at least
he could exchange a little conversation with this one and
that. He probably had more conversation than he had had
at home with the late and much-occupied Harriet. His son
and daughter-in-law had taken him and Janey to their house
for a family Christmas dinner and a Tree – a thing which the
late Harriet had gladly abandoned as soon as her children
would let her. So the two younger people, along with others
belonging to other residents, were invited to Deanery
House to join the party. And Harold's came. 'You have such
nice children,' said Maria Bowater to Janey Peters, forgetting,
in the haze of goodwill and sherry, that Janey was not Harold's
wife.

Janey reflected on her destiny. Always somebody's helpmeet but nobody's wife. Except for a few days in World
War One which were not worth counting. Any pick-up
could have played her part in those few days, which had been
mostly spent in bed.

The Brandling cats, displaying more dudgeon than grief
at being deserted (which in fact they were not – the younger
Brandling family would have seen to their welfare), took off to
the barns and woods, where no doubt some of them would be
shot by those sportsmen who took a poor view of cats in
relation to the tame poults of hand-reared pheasants. The
remaining orphan was Janey Peters's car, which she could not
bring herself to sell. She lent it to the Brandling daughter-in-
law, who would give it a happy and useful home and might
be inspired to take Harold and Janey out for short drives
in it, come the summer. If they were still alive.

It was all drawing to a close for Janey, the good and the
bad, and oddly enough the diminuendo into old age seemed
better than much that had gone before. Responsibility had
been lifted from her shoulders. She could go to the Public

Library and take as long as she liked to choose books, she could sit in a café with Maria Bowater, wasting time pleasantly until it was necessary to dawdle on their walking-sticks back to Deanery House for luncheon. Then the afternoon rest, oh, what a luxury. She hoped that Harold too was contented but of course he would not say. He had never said much at any time. Words, in any meaningful sequence, anything beyond Yes and No, had been as hard to extract from him as teeth, the late Harriet used to say. 'I can so easily bamboozle him with words,' she used to say; 'it's a shame really.'

On New Year's Eve there was a dance at the Radmere Corn Hall. That is to say a jiggle-joggling pack of bodies jiggle-joggled in a howling storm of sound. (They had given up calling it music, 'sound' was the word, the Three Bears Sound, the Village Sound, the Highwaymen's Sound.)

Two muffled figures, enlaced, escaped unnoticed from the din and walked towards the church. There they sat down on one of the long stone benches inside the porch. Sanford and Janice had never been parted for more than a fortnight, in summer holidays, since their school lives began but now an imminent and much longer parting had to be faced.

They clung together on the cold stone seat.

'I wish we were going to the same place. Durham and Essex could hardly be farther apart,' said Sanford.

'Except Sussex, or Exeter,' said Janice with a sad little giggle. Sanford was the one who was going to Durham. Neither of them knew the North of England at all.

There was a silence. Then Janice said, 'It's not for ever. We'll get home in the holidays.'

'It'll have to be hitch-hiking for me,' said the boy, 'but please not for you, Jan, it's not safe for girls.'

'My parents will fork out the rail fare if they want to see me,' said Janice, 'and probably they'd be ashamed not to,

but I'm not their favourite person because I won't be a
doctor or a nurse.'

'A teacher's just as important.'

'Not to them. They're very basic. Health comes before
frills like Eng. Lang. and Lit. Well, he's a doc and she was a
hospital Sister. They call me the Soft Option. But I'll show
'em.'

'There's my girl!' said Sanford, clutching her to his side
and kissing her chin.

'I've sometimes wondered,' she whispered.

'Oh, Jan, you *knew*. But it's only common sense to hold
back a bit, we're so young, we've no money and no work and
no degrees to get work *with*, and you get into such muddles
if you – '

'I know, love, I know.'

'If I got you a little ring – it'd have to be a cheap one,
just a sham stone – would you wear it?'

'A curtain ring would do,' she laughed, happy now.

'This old stone is darn' cold to the sit-upon,' said Sanford,
also cheered by having settled so important a matter. 'We
ought to be getting back for the Old Lang Syne bit.'

So, interlaced again, they walked back slowly to the Corn
Hall.

Colin was there, to report the function, and with him was
the girl-cub, fresh from school, engaged by the other paper
to replace Aubrey Stiff immediately upon his resignation
(nobody but his parents yet knew he was dead). She was a
bright kid with a good O-level in English: she had left
school at sixteen because her parents wanted her to earn her
keep. Maybe it won't hurt her, said Colin to himself, if she
can stick it. I started out the same way.

To her he said, 'There'll be times when you're bored to
screaming. The same things over and over again every year.
Weddings, funerals, flower shows, prize-givings, school

plays. Over and over again. Lists of names, that's what the readers want, to see their names in print, that's why seven different relatives will pay good money to put the name of the same person, father, uncle, cousin or whatever he may be to them, seven times in the Deaths column of the county papers. A status symbol. He hasn't died seven times, but their family name has appeared seven times. Names, don't you forget – '

'Do they really do that?'

'They do. Shows you the importance of names. And you get them right or you'll hear about it. I'll let you have my list of the organizers of this shindig and the winners of the competitions. It's boring for us because we don't know them, they're robots, all we know about them is that they do the same things over and over again. But keep with it, because once in a way – ' and a slight shudder passed through him at the memory – 'once in a way it all comes alive, you know it's real, not a stupid repetitive charade. You've *learnt* something.'

The little girl, who had rich brown hair, and brown eyes which spectacles enhanced instead of spoiling, grinned at him. 'You give me hope,' she said. 'I'll keep with it.'

Then they both had to leave the 'Press table' and find places in one of the circles for the singing of Auld Lang Syne: and the New Year emerged from the wings just as the old one had, same place, same time, last year. Globally speaking, the promise was rather worse: locally, much as before.